THE LOST TREASURE OF
FERNANDO MONTOYA

THE DAVIS DETECTIVE MYSTERIES

THE LOST TREASURE OF
FERNANDO MONTOYA

RICK ACKER

Kregel
Publications

The Lost Treasure of Fernando Montoya

Published by Kregel Publications, a division of Kregel, Inc., P.O. Box 2607, Grand Rapids, MI 49501.

Cover illustration: Kevin Ingram

ISBN 0-8254-2005-9

Printed in the United States of America

1 2 3 4 5 / 07 06 05 04 03

Do not store up for yourselves treasures on earth, where moth and rust destroy, and where thieves break in and steal. But store up for yourselves treasures in heaven, where moth and rust do not destroy, and where thieves do not break in and steal. For where your treasure is, there your heart will be also.

—Matthew 6:19–21 NIV

THE LOST TREASURE OF
FERNANDO MONTOYA

CHAPTER 1

A SMALL FIRE IN A BIG HOUSE

The intruder looked out over the lawn of Jim Franklin's Pacific Heights mansion. A scattering of people walked alone or stood in groups of two or three on the broad expanse of grass between the marble veranda and the street.

After a few minutes, the people gathered for a brief outdoor memorial led by Rev. Fishburn, the pastor of the church the Franklins attended. The intruder knew the memorial would take only ten minutes, and that wasn't much time. The crowd turned to face Rev. Fishburn. Their backs were all to the house and they blocked the pastor's view, so none of them saw the dark shadow flit from a clump of rosebushes by the driveway to the south door. The intruder quickly forced the latch on the door and went in.

Heart beating like a hammer, the dark figure walked quickly through the huge, empty house. The rich Persian rugs on the floors silenced all footsteps, but there was still a terrible risk that someone would glance through a window at the wrong moment. Every time a floorboard squeaked or a shutter creaked in the light wind outside, the figure froze.

Eight minutes left. The intruder found Jim Franklin's study and opened the door as quietly as possible—its old hinges groaned loudly—and slipped into the musty old room. It still smelled like cigar smoke, even though it had been months since Mr. Franklin had last smoked in there. A book lay open on his desk and the chair was pushed back, as if the old man had just left to go get something and would be back any minute. The intruder involuntarily glanced back at the door as if expecting him to come walking in.

He wouldn't, of course. He had died a week ago from a burst blood vessel. He had been ill for some time, but his death had taken most people by surprise. It had also left some unfinished business in a safe in the study wall.

The intruder had seen him open it several times and remembered the combination: 17-12-49. The dark figure's gloved fingers dialed it, but the safe didn't open. Maybe the first two numbers were out of order. The clock on the desk showed six minutes left. The gloved fingers shook with panic as they tried again.

Click. The handle turned. The intruder sighed with relief, then pulled open the heavy steel and brass door and looked into the safe's darkly shadowed interior.

There it was! The corner of an old document poked out from under a stack of stock certificates. The burglar pulled it out and leafed through it quickly. Its pages were covered with spidery old-fashioned handwriting, and age had turned the once-white paper to the color of yellowed bones. Yes, this was it. The dark figure shut the safe and walked quickly out of the study and toward the living room, carrying the antique pages cautiously between a gloved thumb and forefinger as if they were something dangerous or disgusting.

Four minutes left. The intruder began to sweat, even though

the house was cold. For one panicked instant, the burglar considered running back to the study, putting the papers back, and sneaking out of the house as if nothing had happened. The figure stood wavering for an instant before starting forward again. In just a few more minutes—three and a half to be exact—everything would be fine.

The last time the intruder had seen Mr. Franklin's living room, it had been filled with people who were there to celebrate another successful acquisition by the Franklin Company. Everyone had been laughing and talking happily, and a big warm fire had crackled and snapped merrily in the massive marble fireplace. Now the huge room was filled with emptiness and shadows, and the fireplace was cold and dark and looked like the mouth of a cave.

Three minutes left. The intruder walked softly and soundlessly across the wide wooden floor toward the fireplace, a shadow among shadows. The masked head turned quickly from left to right, glancing around one last time to make sure no one was looking. A cigarette lighter appeared from a hidden pocket, and the burglar lit the bottom corner of the papers from the safe. The flames started slowly, then suddenly leaped up hungrily toward the gloved hand.

The figure hurriedly dropped the burning pages into the fireplace, then watched with satisfaction and growing relief as they charred and disintegrated into glowing ash. The little fire was dwarfed by the giant fireplace and gave almost no heat, but it warmed the burglar's heart.

One minute left. All that was left was a little pile of feathery gray ash. The intruder stirred it with a poker until it no longer looked like paper ash, then took the fireplace broom and brushed the dusty pile toward the back of the fireplace, where it mingled with the remains of older and less important fires.

Out of time. Rev. Fishburn, who was surprisingly short-winded for a pastor, had actually finished his remarks thirty seconds early. The small crowd outside began to disperse, and a couple of the guests had just made their way up onto the veranda, where they could see into the living room. The burglar froze in a half crouch by the fireplace. An elderly woman in a blue dress glanced in through the window, her eyes idly wandering over the furniture and artwork as she chatted with a friend. The intruder stayed absolutely motionless, hoping desperately that the old woman wouldn't notice the shadowy figure lurking by the poker stand.

The woman looked here and there in the room for what seemed like an eternity, her gaze resting on a piece of furniture or a painting or nothing at all. Then she looked straight at the burglar. Her smile didn't fade and she didn't stop chatting, but her eyes stopped moving. The intruder stopped breathing as the woman squinted slightly, as if she was trying to make out the strange dark shape in the shadows.

Seconds ticked by as the old woman peered at the shadowy figure in the dark room. The burglar was about to make a dash for the door, but the woman apparently decided it was nothing and walked away with her friend.

The intruder, finally able to move again, stole out of the room and slipped back out the south door. Inside the empty house, the warm spot on the fireplace floor gradually cooled, and the last clue that anyone had been in the house that day vanished.

CHAPTER 2

AN OLD MYSTERY

As Arthur and Kirstin Davis made their way out of the airport gate, they scanned the crowd of waiting faces for Connie Hoghton, who was male in spite of his name. His real name was Conable, but he was too young (thirty-five) and too much fun to be called that. When he had played football in high school and college, his teammates had called him "Cannibal" because he would eat opposing quarterbacks for lunch. If he had turned pro after college, people might still call him that, but a knee injury had turned him from a linebacker into an accountant—and Cannibal is not a very good name for an accountant.

Connie was Arthur's and Kirstin's favorite uncle. He was their mother's younger brother, and they would be spending a month of their summer break with him while their parents took a long vacation cruise in the Caribbean. Their mom and dad had felt guilty about leaving Arthur and Kirstin behind, but the thought of spending a month in San Francisco with Uncle Connie was much more exciting to Arthur and Kirstin than spending a month on a floating hotel with their parents.

Connie was a big man, and Arthur and Kirstin almost immediately spotted his blond head sticking up above the rest of the crowd, a broad smile splitting his tan face as he waved to them. They waved back and made their way over to him.

"Welcome to San Francisco! It's great to see you guys again!" he said as he gave Kirstin a hug and shook Arthur's hand warmly.

"It's great to see you too, Uncle Connie," returned Arthur. He pushed his sandy brown hair out of his eyes and stretched. Sitting in cramped airplane seats always made his long arms and legs stiff.

"Yeah," added Kirstin. "Thanks for inviting us."

"No problem. It's always fun to have guests. It gives me an excuse to get out a little." Uncle Connie had already promised them that they could hike in Yosemite, windsurf on the Bay, and climb Coit Tower. And that was just the first week.

"Say, are you two tired from the flight?"

"Uh, not really," answered Arthur, not quite sure what Connie was getting at. Kirstin shook her head.

"A friend of mine has three extra tickets to see the Giants play the Cubs tonight at Pac Bell Park. Want to go?"

"Sure!" said Arthur, and Kirstin nodded. Kirstin wasn't a huge baseball fan, but she had been to two games at Wrigley Field in Chicago and had enjoyed herself. Arthur, on the other hand, loved baseball (and the Cubs) almost as much as soccer; he had already spent several long summer afternoons talking to the TV set during close games.

"Terrific!" said Connie.

"We'll drop off your stuff at my condo and head straight to the game. It starts in an hour."

Pac Bell Park is a big red brick building that looks old, but isn't. It sits so close to the edge of a cove that if the batter hits a home run over the right field fence, it lands in the water. In fact, boaters crowd close to the stadium on game days, hoping to catch a home run ball. Some people even bring specially trained dogs to swim after balls.

Inside the park, Arthur and Kirstin found gift shops, news-stands, and especially restaurants. "Ever had garlic fries?" Connie asked. They hadn't, so he bought them each a box of fries and a Coke, and they headed for their seats.

Connie's friend was already there. A fit, handsome man about Connie's age stood up and put out his hand for Connie to shake. He looked small next to Connie, but then most people did. A pretty woman with red hair, green eyes, and perfect makeup also stood as they approached.

"Michael, I'd like you to meet my niece and nephew, Kirstin and Arthur Davis. Arthur and Kirstin, this is my good client and good friend, Michael Franklin. He owns a little family business you may have heard of; it's called the Franklin Company."

Kirstin's eyes grew round and Arthur said, "Wow!" The Franklin Company made bikes, bike helmets, scooters, and basically everything else that had to do with foot-powered transportation. Franklin bikes were the best you could buy, and they were minor status symbols at Arthur and Kirstin's high school, where Arthur was a junior and Kirstin was a freshman.

Kirstin recovered first from the surprise of being in the presence of *the* Mr. Franklin. "Nice to meet you, Mr. Franklin," she said politely and shook his hand. "I'm saving up for one of your bikes. They're really great."

"They are great bikes," confirmed Arthur as he shook Mr. Franklin's hand. "Thanks for inviting us to the game."

"I'm glad you could make it on such short notice," replied Mr. Franklin with a friendly smile that made little crinkles around his blue eyes. "And please call me Michael." He turned to the redheaded woman with him. "Let me introduce my fiancée, Tricia Franklin."

Michael Franklin enjoyed the look of confusion on Arthur's and Kirstin's faces for a moment, then explained, "Tricia is my third cousin, that's why we have the same last name. We have a great-great-grandfather named Theodore Franklin in common. In fact, he's the one who founded the company."

"Neat," said Kirstin. "So does your whole family live in California?"

Tricia shook her head. "Actually, my great-grandfather, Theodore's son, sold his stock in the bicycle business to his brother—"

"My great-grandfather," interrupted Michael.

"Yes," said Tricia. "Anyway, he decided that bicycles were just a fad that wouldn't last. So he sold his stock and moved back east to New York."

"Where he invested in a horse and buggy company," chimed in Michael with an amused smile. "It was the same year Henry Ford started making Model T cars."

Tricia smiled and said, "Well, everybody makes mistakes."

"Like that," said Arthur, who had been glancing at the game and winced as the Cubs' shortstop let a grounder dribble between his legs.

They turned to watching the game and eating garlic fries for a while, both of which Arthur enjoyed immensely. It was a close game with good hitting and bad pitching, which makes for exciting baseball.

Even exciting baseball bored Kirstin after about half an hour though. She tried to make conversation with Arthur and Connie, but they were too distracted by the game.

Kirstin's attention drifted from the game to the crowd watching it. She noticed a little boy five rows down who looked like he was about two. He seemed to be meticulously scraping something off the seat next to him. His back was turned to his parents, who were watching the game pretty intently. The little boy stood up triumphantly with a wad of old chewing gum in his hand and shoved it in his mouth. "Eewww!" exclaimed Kirstin.

Tricia laughed and said, "You saw that too, huh? Pretty gross."

"It sure is," agreed Kirstin. The boy's parents had noticed him chewing and were now trying to get the gum out of his mouth.

"Michael and I have something to look forward to when we have kids," said Tricia, shaking her head.

"Are you guys getting married soon?" asked Kirstin.

Tricia nodded. "In August. I'm the in-house lawyer at the Franklin Company, but my real job for the last couple of months has been wedding planner. It's been fun, but I'll be glad when it's over."

"You must be really busy," commented Kirstin.

"I am," agreed Tricia, "but that's OK. Being really busy isn't too bad if you're doing something that's mostly fun, and I've had fun planning the wedding. So, what do you do for fun, Kirstin?"

"Let's see," Kirstin answered. "I ride horses and Arthur and I have youth group once a week. Other than that, I go out with friends and stuff. Oh, and Arthur and I run a detective agency, but we're not working on any cases right now."

That caught Michael's attention. "Detective agency?" he asked with raised eyebrows. "Hey, are you two the brother and sister detectives that Connie told me about?"

"That's us," said Kirstin.

"How would you like to look into an old mystery for me?"

"What's it about?"

"Let's just say I'd like you to solve the case of the lost treasure of Fernando Montoya."

Tricia turned to him with an appalled look. "They're on vacation, Michael. I'm sure the last thing they'll want to do is spend their time in the library looking through dusty old books and newspapers."

"Actually, it sounds interesting," Kirstin said. A month is a long time for a vacation, and she had been wondering what they would do while Connie was at work during the week. Tricia's comment about dusty books worried her though. She'd rather be bored on the beach than bored in a library basement. "Could you tell me a little more about it?"

"Sure," he said. "To make a long story short, the Franklin who founded my company had a friend who lost some gold—actually a lot of gold—during the Gold Rush.

"My assistant is related to him. In fact, her family has been with the company ever since it was founded. She had asked me once if I knew what had happened to her great-great-great-grandfather's gold. I didn't know, but I promised her I'd look into it. It was sort of a present for her long service. She's worked at the company for twenty years, mostly as my father's assistant. When he passed away a couple of months ago, she started working for me. She's always done a terrific job for us, so I thought this would be a little way I could say thank you."

"I think it'd be fun to investigate it," said Kirstin, "but let me talk to my brother first."

She leaned over and nudged Arthur, who was completely sucked into the game. She explained the case to him in an excited whisper, but he didn't seem very interested. In fact, he didn't even turn toward her while she was talking. That was just as well, she decided, because he had been eating *a lot* of garlic fries. When she finished, all he said was, "Uh, yeah sure. Sounds great."

Kirstin turned back to Michael. "We'll take the case."

"Great!" he replied. "How much do you charge?"

"Twenty dollars an hour?" said Kirstin tentatively. Usually she and Arthur just charged a flat amount—say thirty dollars—to find a lost dog or catch a locker thief, but this job sounded much bigger.

"So forty dollars an hour for the two of you, plus expenses, right?" said Michael.

"Sure," said Kirstin. That was actually double what she had meant, but she wasn't going to complain.

"Deal!" said Michael, and he shook her hand with a broad smile on his face. "I'm out of town for the rest of the week, but why don't you stop by my office at 9:30 Monday morning so I can give you some more details?"

"We'll be there," said Kirstin enthusiastically. Finding a treasure from the days of the Wild West, now *that* was her idea of a fun vacation!

CHAPTER 3

THE LOST CITY

Kirstin was beginning to regret accepting Connie's suggestion that they stop on the way to Yosemite and hike back to a "lost city" for a picnic lunch. It had sounded interesting, but she hadn't realized it would involve getting so sweaty. The long, dry grass rustled as she waded through it, struggling up a hill that was much higher and steeper than it had looked from the road. The sun was bright and hot overhead, and her wet hair stuck to her neck. She was breathing hard, and she could feel her feet sweating in the thick socks and hiking boots Connie had made them wear.

Even Arthur, who was on the varsity soccer team at their high school, was a little out of breath by the time they reached the top. Connie took a deep breath, stretched out his arm grandly, and said, "Behold the Lost City of Johnsonville!"

"Where?" said Arthur, shading his eyes with his hand as he scanned the landscape. All he could see was rolling hills of golden brown grass, three trees, and two bored-looking cows.

Connie grinned. "I'll show you," he said as he started down the far side of the hill. "That's city hall," he said, pointing to a nondescript pile of rocks. "You can see what's left of the stone chimney." He pointed to some more rocks. "There's the general store. The church was right next to it. Look, you can still see some of the gravestones." They walked over and looked at the small, weathered markers. "Elijah Hunter, January 15, 1785 – February 6, 1852," Arthur read, tracing the letters with his finger. "I'll bet old Elijah won't recognize his hometown when the Resurrection comes."

Connie and Kirstin laughed. They sat down on the remains of a stone wall in the town square and had their lunch. Connie had packed chips and his special jalapeño-baloney-cheddar-sourdough sandwiches, and lots of root beer and Coke to wash them down. Kirstin had tasted Connie's sandwiches before and therefore just packed some fruit for herself.

"How many people were there in Johnsonville?" Kirstin asked as they ate.

"About fifteen or twenty thousand," answered Connie. "That was a pretty big city for California back then."

"What happened to them?" she asked.

"Johnsonville was a tent city. Virtually everybody lived in shacks and canvas tents, and there were only a few real buildings. I've already shown you most of them. Johnsonville appeared less than a month after gold was found in Johnson's Creek," he gestured toward a brown little stream that meandered through a gully along the edge of the ruins, "and it disappeared within two months after the gold ran out. Aside from Elijah Hunter and his neighbors in the churchyard, the only people left were a few rancheros who used these hills to graze their cattle."

Arthur shaded his eyes and squinted at the hills and dells around them. After a few seconds he said, "So where are the gold mines?"

"Most people just sluiced or panned for gold in the stream," explained Connie, "but there's an abandoned pit mine right around that hill." He pointed to a low, grassy hummock. "Want to go see it?"

They got up and worked their way through the thick grass and weeds toward the hill Connie had indicated. It was hotter now, and the sun was almost straight overhead. All three of them were sweating, and Kirstin wished she had ignored Connie and left those stupid, hot, heavy hiking boots behind. Gym shoes would be *so* much more comfortable right now.

The mine was a giant lumpy hole next to the creek. Its bottom was green and marshy, probably from water leaking in from the stream. Its sides were full of smaller holes, gouges, and what looked like the mouths of tunnels. Old piles of dirt and rock lay everywhere. Even at high noon, it was full of shadows and mysterious-looking dark places.

Arthur scrambled down to explore, and Kirstin followed after him. "I'm getting too old for this kind of thing," said Connie as he sat down in the shade of a small tree. "You guys be careful. Don't go in any tunnels."

"OK!" Arthur called back as they picked their way down the side of the hole. At the bottom, Kirstin bent down to look at a bed of tiny, but perfect, white and purple wildflowers. Then she discovered a bright red salamander crawling along the side of a little pool.

She walked slowly across the mine floor, stopping every few steps to look at the wildlife that covered the ground like a living carpet. She noticed a six-foot-long snakeskin lying on a sunbaked rock and called out, "Hey, Arthur! Check this out!"

He didn't answer. She looked up and saw him standing a

few feet into a tunnel with his back turned to her. He was only about twenty yards away, so he must have heard her. "Hey, Arthur!" she called again.

He ignored her again and took a slow baby step backward. "This is weird," she said to herself. She jogged over to Arthur. He didn't look up even though she called his name again. He just stared into the shadows and took another small step back.

For the first time, Kirstin noticed a strange buzzing noise coming from the tunnel. Her eyes adjusted to the darkness of the shadow—and she saw a huge rattlesnake just a few feet in front of her brother!

She could make out the snake's long body, coiled in thick loops beside a rock. Its big triangle-shaped head was raised and pulled back, ready to strike. It was perfectly still, except for the rattle on its tail, which shook so fast it was a blur. That was the buzzing sound she heard.

Kirstin screamed. Arthur twitched. And the snake's head whipped forward quick as lightning and sank its fangs into Arthur's ankle!

CHAPTER 4

THE EMERGENCY ROOM

Arthur yelled and jumped back. He stumbled and fell sprawling on the hill outside the tunnel's mouth. A little avalanche of stones and dust tumbled the few feet to the mine floor, followed by Arthur.

Connie's head appeared over the edge of the mine just as Arthur landed and Kirstin screamed again. "Hold on!" he yelled.

Connie ignored the twisting path Arthur and Kirstin had taken. Instead, he came running and jumping down the near-vertical side of the mine, completely disregarding his own safety in his hurry to reach Arthur.

About three-quarters of the way down, a rock gave way under Connie's foot and his leg collapsed under him. He grimaced and grabbed his knee, but he got back on his feet and hobbled over to Arthur and Kirstin as best he could.

Arthur made sure he was safely away from the cave, pulled off his boot and sock and was examining his ankle by the time Connie arrived. Fortunately, the snake's fangs hadn't gone all the way through the thick leather and padding of Arthur's boot. In fact, the tip of one fang had broken off and stuck out of the boot like a venomous thorn.

"Are you OK?" Connie asked.

"Yeah," said Arthur. "A rattlesnake tried to bite me, but these boots kept his fangs from getting through. Now I see why you told us to wear them." Kirstin was suddenly very glad she hadn't worn gym shoes after all.

Arthur noticed the pain in his uncle's face and how he was putting all his weight on his left leg. "Hey, are *you* OK?" he asked.

"Actually, no," said Connie. "I think I tore up my right knee coming down here." He tried putting some weight on his injured leg and nearly fell. "I did. Can you give me a hand?"

"Should we call 911?" asked Kirstin worriedly.

Connie shook his head. "Are you kidding? We're out in the middle of nowhere; an ambulance will take forever to get here."

Arthur and Kirstin helped their uncle back to the car. They decided that Connie would lean on Arthur while Kirstin carried all of their picnic gear. It was a slow, sweaty, and dirty process for all of them. It was also very painful for Connie, but there was nothing anybody could do about that.

Connie had to go to the hospital, of course. There was one just a few blocks from his apartment, and he decided he'd rather go there than try to look for something closer to Johnsonville. His injured knee made it impossible for him to drive, so Arthur had to drive them back into San Francisco. Connie's car had a stick shift transmission, which he explained briefly to Arthur through gritted teeth. But having something explained to you and being able to do it right the first time are not always the same thing, and they weren't for Arthur now. The trip back was full of sudden speed changes and the awful sound of grinding gears as Arthur struggled with his uncle's expensive imported car.

Arthur could see Connie wincing in the rearview mirror. "Is it your knee or my driving?" he asked.

"Both," groaned his uncle. "The last time my knee felt this bad, I had surgery and was out of commission for six weeks." Arthur shifted gears just then, but forgot to step on the clutch in time. The car jumped and sounds of protest came from the transmission.

"Sorry," said Arthur sheepishly.

"That's OK," said Connie. "I probably would have had to replace the transmission at some point anyway." They drove in silence for half a minute. "Really," Connie continued with an effort, "don't worry about it. I know you're doing the best you can."

After a drive that seemed to last forever came a wait in the hospital emergency room that lasted even longer, at least for Arthur and Kirstin. A nurse had come to take Connie away for testing almost as soon as they arrived, but the detectives had nothing to do but sit in the emergency room lobby and wait. And wait. Finally, a nurse came to take them up to Connie's hospital room.

"They're doing some tests, but it looks like I'm stuck here for tonight at least," he said as he pulled out his wallet and gave Kirstin a ten dollar bill.

"You guys catch a cab home. I'm going to try to get some rest as soon as those painkillers get here."

Kirstin noticed how drawn his face was and realized he must have been in serious pain for the past two hours.

"OK, Uncle Connie," she said, "we'll come visit you tomorrow morning."

"Hope you feel better soon," added Arthur.

"Oh, do you want me to take your car home for you? It's in a parking spot with a two-hour limit."

"No, no," said Connie quickly. "That's OK. I'll call one of my friends and have them take care of it." The nurse came to give him a shot, and Arthur and Kirstin said goodbye.

When they came to visit Connie the next morning, both good news and bad news awaited them. The good news was that Connie was feeling much better and wouldn't need surgery. The bad news was that he would be flat on his back for the next week and would be on crutches for three weeks after that. For the rest of the vacation, Arthur and Kirstin would be on their own.

ON THE CASE

At 8:45 Monday morning, Arthur was sitting in Connie's kitchen wearing old sweatpants and a T-shirt. The morning sunlight brightened the air and glowed softly on the floor and countertops, and a few sailboats were out on San Francisco Bay. Arthur was just getting ready to start on a second bowl of Cap'n Crunch. He stretched comfortably, sat down, and picked up his spoon.

Kirstin walked in and stared at him, her blue eyes round with horror. "Arthur, what are you doing?"

He gave her a puzzled look and said, "I'm eating breakfast. Why?"

"Because we have to leave to see Michael Franklin in fifteen minutes!"

"Why are we seeing Michael Franklin?"

"To talk about the case!"

"What case?"

"The case I told you about at the baseball game!"

He looked at her blankly for a second, then said, "Oh, was that what you kept bothering me about when the bases were loaded in the seventh inning?"

She thought of so many things to say all at once that none

of them could come out. "Well," Arthur continued, "you can tell me about it on the way over." He got up to go take a shower. He stopped at the bathroom door and looked back at the kitchen wistfully. "I can't believe you're making me waste perfectly good cereal like this. That was really bad planning." Then he shut the door before she could say anything.

Fifty-three minutes later, they were hurrying through the executive office suite of the Franklin Company. They were in the original Franklin Building, a square limestone structure set on top of a large hill, so that even the windows on the ground floor had spectacular views. Antique bicycles and old pictures hung on the wooden walls in the wide, plushly carpeted hallways. Kirstin thought it looked like a private museum owned by someone very rich, then realized that was probably at least partly what it was.

They found Michael's secretary's desk, and Arthur said they were there to see him. Kirstin added, "And please tell him we're sorry we're late." She threw a quick glance at Arthur to make it clear that *she* was not the one who had been late.

The secretary, a large Hispanic woman of about forty with a strong, square face, smiled in amusement. "Actually, if I don't say anything, he'll never know you weren't on time. He's spent the last hour on a conference call that was supposed to take fifteen minutes. Have a seat, and I'll let him know you're here." She wrote a note on a piece of paper and took it into Michael's office. She emerged a minute later and said, "He'll be with you in five minutes."

They sat down in a small waiting area outside his office. Kirstin glanced at the secretary's desk and noticed that her nameplate said "Olivia Montoya." She nudged Arthur and made a small gesture toward the desk. "Check out the name-plate," she whispered.

Arthur checked it out. He remembered what Kirstin had said about there still being some Montoyas who worked for the Franklin Company. He leaned over to Kirstin and whispered, "Do you think she's—" He didn't bother finishing his sentence because Kirstin was nodding vigorously.

"Excuse me, Ms. Montoya?" Arthur asked awkwardly. "Are you, uh, related to Fernando Montoya, the gold prospector?"

She looked startled for a second, then said, "Why yes, he was my great-great-great-grandfath—" She stopped and stared at Arthur and Kirstin. "Are you two the detectives Michael hired?"

"Yes, we are," answered Kirstin, her voice sounding a little more defensive than she had meant it to. She hated it when people assumed that just because she and Arthur were still in high school, they couldn't be real detectives.

If Olivia noticed Kirstin's tone, she didn't show it. "Good luck! Finding that treasure would be even better than winning the lottery."

Just then the door to Michael's office opened and he stepped out. Kirstin had expected him to be wearing a suit, like their father always did in the office, but he had on a red polo shirt and khaki pants. For a moment, Kirstin thought he must not take his job seriously, but then she realized she hadn't seen a single suit during their cab ride through San Francisco's business district. "Hi, Kirstin. Hi, Arthur," Michael said as he warmly shook their hands and escorted them into his office.

The office was a big room with a high ceiling and dark wood-paneled walls. It had an awkward new and old feeling to it that both Arthur and Kirstin noticed. A massive antique wood desk and leather chair stood at one end with an arched window behind them. In the middle of the room, however, were a modern glass and steel table and matching chairs. Old pictures of bearded men wearing uncomfortable-looking suits hung on the walls, but so did framed posters from the Giants' last World Series appearance.

"Have a seat," said Michael, gesturing to the glass and steel table. He walked over to his desk and said, "Olivia," he paused, "could you come in here please? I'd like you to sit in on this meeting."

Ms. Montoya's voice floated down to them from somewhere near the ceiling. "I'll be there in just a minute."

Michael smiled as Arthur and Kirstin looked up to find out where her voice was coming from. They didn't see anything. "Do you like my speakerphone?" he asked. "It's voice activated, so all I have to do is say someone's name and then be quiet for a second and it will automatically dial their number. Then I can have a conversation with them just as if they were in the room with me."

"That's really cool," said Kirstin, who imagined how much fun it would be to have a system like that in her room at home.

"It is, isn't it?" said Michael, still smiling happily. "I put it in when I moved to this office a month ago. This," he gestured at the room around him, "has been the president's office for almost a hundred years. It was my great-grandfather's office, my grandfather's, and my father's." As he listed the previous occupants, he pointed to the portraits on the wall. He paused for a moment as he looked at his father's brand new portrait. "Now it's mine."

Just then, Ms. Montoya walked in. "Showing off your new phone, Michael?" she asked with a smile.

He took a deep breath and smiled back. "Yeah." He turned to Arthur and Kirstin. "It's eerie. She can read my mind."

"Either that or I know when there are people in your office who haven't seen it yet."

"We'd better get this meeting started, hadn't we?" he said as he started over to the table. Arthur and Kirstin followed him and they all sat down.

Ms. Montoya nodded. "You have a 10:30 call, so we only have about twenty-five minutes."

They all sat down, and Michael pulled out a big accordion folder full of yellowed paper. He put it down on the table with a thump. "I had our records department pull every piece of paper they could find in our files mentioning Fernando Montoya or his gold, and this is what they found. I haven't had a chance to go through it in any detail, but I thought it might give you a start." He pushed the folder over to them, and Arthur started flipping through it. There were lots of ancient bank statements, invoices, incomprehensible legal documents, and similarly boring items.

Arthur closed the folder and put it aside, bitterly regretting that he had apparently promised to spend his San Francisco vacation reading through all this junk. This was the *last* time he'd let his sister ask him questions while he was watching an exciting ballgame—there was no telling what he might later find out he'd agreed to do.

CHAPTER 6

GOLD!

"Now let me tell you what I know about old Fernando, his gold, and Ted Franklin, my great-great-grandfather," began Michael Franklin.

"Great-great-grandpa Ted was working in a steel mill in New York in 1849 when he saw a newspaper with a huge headline screaming 'GOLD!' He bought it and read that gold had been discovered in California. He quit his job the next day and headed West to go prospecting. He didn't have enough money to make the trip on his own, so he teamed up with another man who had caught the gold bug. His name was Obadiah Washington, and he had more money than my great-great-grandpa Ted, but he was willing to share if Ted would help him get through Kansas."

"Why did he need help to get through Kansas?" asked Arthur.

"Well, Obadiah was a freed slave, and Kansas was split pretty evenly between people who supported slavery and people who opposed it. They hated each other, and the pro-slavery people hated freed slaves.

"Obadiah knew he would have to go through Kansas to get to California because there was no good way around it unless he could afford a berth on a ship from New York to San Francisco, which he couldn't. So he looked for a partner. Ted was only sixteen, but he was big and strong for his age and had a reputation around the mill as a good fighter.

"They actually made it through Kansas pretty easily. They avoided the pro-slavery areas and stayed off the roads after dark. Some churches and abolitionist towns even gave them free meals and places to sleep. It wasn't until the Rocky Mountains that they ran into serious trouble."

"Apaches?" asked Kirstin. In May her history class had done a unit on the Western tribes and their conflicts with settlers.

He shook his head. "Scarlet fever. They spent the winter in a tent city outside Fort Bridger, in the middle of the mountains. Scarlet fever broke out in the camp, and they both came down with it. Ted recovered, but Obadiah didn't. Ted buried his body in a local graveyard and headed West again in the spring with some other men from the camp."

"Why didn't he go back to his family in New York? I mean, wasn't he scared to go on by himself?" asked Kirstin. She imagined Arthur—who was the same age now as Ted was then—striking out across the Wild West with a bunch of men he hardly knew.

Michael shrugged. "He probably was, but going back wouldn't have been any easier. Besides, he still wanted to make his fortune in the California gold fields."

"Did he?" asked Arthur.

"We'll get to that in a minute," Michael said with a smile. "They got to San Francisco by late spring and they all went their separate ways. Ted wanted to go prospecting, but he didn't have any good ideas on where to go. He knew the places where people had already found gold, but those spots—and all the areas around them—were already claimed.

"So he needed another partner, someone who knew the area well and could help him find a good spot to start panning or digging. Most people like that were, of course, already out prospecting. Lots of men claimed to know just where to dig if only they could find a partner with money for supplies, but Ted couldn't find anyone he really trusted.

"Then after church one Sunday, he was talking to a local fellow named Fernando Montoya. Fernando had been a ranch hand until he lost his right arm and part of his right foot in an accident. After that, he had to make ends meet by doing odd jobs around town. His son had to work too, which embarrassed him. He also really missed being out in the countryside, so when he heard that Ted was looking for a partner who knew the lay of the land, he did everything he could to talk Ted into taking him.

"Ted was reluctant at first, but Fernando kept talking about how well he knew the area and how helpful he could be around camp. Finally, Ted agreed to take him. He didn't really believe Fernando would be that useful around camp with his missing arm and bad foot, but he did seem to know Northern California pretty well. Besides, Ted was getting desperate.

"Ted was right about Fernando not being able to do many camp chores. It also took them about twice as long as it should have to get to the gold fields because Fernando wasn't very steady on a horse.

"But Fernando was right about knowing the countryside. All of the other prospectors were panning for gold in the valley streams or digging random holes in the ground. Fernando took

Ted up into the hills to where he remembered seeing an overgrown old dry riverbed." He paused for dramatic effect. "They found *over eight hundred pounds* of gold in that riverbed."

"Wow!" gasped Kirstin, trying to picture what it would be like to find that much gold. Then she suddenly realized what must come next in the story. "So, did Ted use his half of the gold to start the Franklin Company?"

He smiled and nodded. "He took a steamer back to San Francisco, wondering what to do with his four hundred pounds of gold. As the ship sailed into port, he noticed a man riding along the docks on a bicycle. Ted had never seen one before, and he was fascinated.

"He found the man with the bicycle as soon as they docked and bought the bike for ten dollars. He spent the next few days figuring out how it worked and riding it around town. By the end of the week, he had fallen in love with bicycles. The rest, of course, is history."

"What happened to Fernando?" asked Arthur.

"No one knows. He disappeared on the trip back. I think he was swept overboard during a storm. We always took care of his family though." He smiled proudly as he thought of his family's charity. "Ted made sure Fernando's widow had a nice house and never needed anything. He gave Fernando's children all good jobs in his bicycle business when they were old enough, and our families have worked together ever since. The Montoyas have all been terrific employees, particularly Olivia." She smiled at the compliment.

"Anyway, Fernando's four hundred pounds of gold never arrived back in San Francisco," Michael continued. "Nobody knows what happened to it. Did he bury it up in the mountains? Was it swept overboard in the storm?" He shrugged. "Nobody knows. For a while, people used to go up into the hills every now and then looking for it. Ted even went once. No one ever found it though."

"Why would Ted go looking for it?" Kirstin asked. "I mean, he traveled back with Fernando, so wouldn't he know what happened to the gold?"

"I remember hearing something about them splitting up," answered Michael. "I'm not sure why or when, but it must have been sometime before Fernando's gold disappeared."

"So it's still out there somewhere, huh?" asked Kirstin.

He shrugged. "Maybe. That's what I want you two to find out. Tell me what happened to the lost treasure of Fernando Montoya. Olivia has volunteered to help you with your investigation." He glanced at a grandfather clock standing against the wall. "I'll have to start getting ready for that call in just a minute. Tricia, my fiancée whom you met at the ball game, has also volunteered to help you. Since you probably don't have access to a car, she said she'd be willing to drive you places. In fact, she volunteered to pick you up after our meeting."

"That's really nice of her," said Arthur.

"She's quite a woman," said Michael with a warm smile. He glanced at the clock again, and Ms. Montoya said, "We'll let you get ready for your call now." She got up, and so did Arthur and Kirstin. They got Ms. Montoya's phone number and e-mail address, said goodbye, and went outside to wait for Tricia.

"It's always so fun to start on a new case," commented Kirstin as they admired the view. To their right, they could see the graceful arches of the Golden Gate Bridge and, in the distance, the green mountains of Marin County. To their left, the hills of San Francisco rolled away to the south, covered with buildings. Each building was different and most were unusual in some way: one was painted orange, another had a little tower sticking out of the top, a third had gargoyles, and so on. It reminded Kirstin a little bit of a picture in a Dr. Seuss book. Straight ahead, the Pacific Ocean lay blue and flat, stretching all the way to China.

"Yeah," responded Arthur as he watched a big ship sail into San Francisco Bay. "It seems a little dull though, don't you think? I'll bet we spend the whole time stuck inside looking through dusty old papers. This is the first case we've worked on where everyone involved has been dead for a hundred years." He looked at the fat folder Michael had given them and sighed. "Oh well, at least we don't have to worry about getting shot at this time," he said.

"Yeah, that's true," said Kirstin. Or so she hoped.

CHAPTER 7

THE "SLASH-AND-GRAB"

Tricia arrived a few minutes later, driving a sporty red Mercedes convertible with the top down. "Hi!" she called as the car pulled up. "Have you two ever seen Pier 39?"

They shook their heads. "This is our first time in San Francisco," said Arthur.

"Well, you can't see San Francisco without seeing Pier 39," she replied. "Hop in!"

Arthur sat in the front seat and Kirstin sat in the back as they made their way through San Francisco's hilly, congested streets. It seemed to Arthur that they probably could have walked faster than they were driving. Certainly he could have run faster. Fortunately, Pier 39 was only a mile and a half from the Franklin Building, so they were there in twenty minutes.

As they sat in a line of barely moving cars, Arthur idly glanced into the door mirror outside his window and noticed a really cool black motorcycle about half a block behind them. Arthur's parents wouldn't let him get a motorcycle, so he was a little jealous of the rider, a muscular man dressed in jeans and a black sleeveless shirt. He wore a black helmet with a tinted visor that hid his face. The motorcycle stayed behind them all the way to Pier 39, never getting closer than half a block or further back than a block.

They parked in a lot two blocks from the pier, and Tricia put the top up on her car. She took off her fashionable black leather jacket and tossed it in the back next to the folder of documents her fiancé had given Arthur and Kirstin.

"Well, there it is," said Tricia, gesturing to a long, wide dock lined with remodeled warehouses. Pier 39 is an old wharf that has been converted into an outdoor mall/theme park/yacht club. For the first half hour or so, Tricia gave them a guided tour. After that, they spent the next two hours exploring Pier 39 together. They wandered through the shops, went on the rides, watched the free street shows (including a man who juggled a bowling ball, a steak knife, and a rubber chicken while telling rapid-fire jokes), and played games in the huge arcades.

They also got to see, hear, and (unfortunately) smell dozens of sea lions on rocks and little floating rafts just off the side of the pier. The animals barked constantly, pushed each other around as each one tried to get a better spot than the others, and instantly fell asleep if they weren't being bothered by their neighbors for five seconds. Kirstin decided she hadn't seen animals that were so funny and so gross at the same time since she watched the baboons at Brookfield Zoo.

At 2:00 in the afternoon, all three of them were sitting on a bench resting their feet and enjoying the afternoon sun. "So, what would you like to do next?" Tricia asked them.

"Actually, maybe we should call it a day," said Kirstin. "I'd like to have a look at those documents this afternoon. Besides, I feel a little bad leaving Uncle Connie alone all day."

"I'm ready to head back too," added Arthur.

They got up and headed back to the car. "So, will you need a ride anywhere tomorrow?" Tricia asked as they walked.

Arthur shrugged. "I don't know. It depends on what's in the documents, I suppose. Can we give you a call tomorrow morning?"

"Sure," said Tricia, "I—"

"Look!" Kirstin yelled, pointing at Tricia's car. A long cut ran from the top right corner of the soft plastic rear window to its bottom left corner. Someone had broken into the car!

"My car!" yelled Tricia and ran over to it.

"Don't touch it! It'll ruin any fingerprints!" called Arthur, but it was too late. Tricia was already holding the sides of the cut open and looking inside. "Oops!" she said and jerked her hands back from the plastic as though it had suddenly become red hot.

Tricia called the police on her cell phone, and she and the two detectives kept back from her convertible as they waited for the squad car to arrive. The parking lot owner, an elderly Chinese man with a heavy accent, came over and apologized to them profusely. He repeated several times that nothing like this had ever happened in his lot before, except once or twice at night. He offered to pay for the window, but Tricia told him not to worry about it since her insurance would cover it.

As Tricia and the lot owner were talking, Arthur noticed a man loading something into the saddlebags of a black motorcycle about half a block away. He was tall and dark-haired, and he had a thick mustache and muscular arms. He looked vaguely familiar, and Arthur realized it was the same man he had seen in his door mirror while they were stuck in traffic on the way to Pier 39.

Just then a police car turned into the lot and drove over to them. The officer got out, wrote down their description of what happened, dusted for fingerprints, and asked them to check the car to tell him what was missing.

Tricia and Arthur went through the car to see if anything was gone. There wasn't really room in the little convertible for Kirstin to help look, so she stood to the side, lost in thought. "I wonder who did this?" she asked herself. *And I wonder if it has anything to do with our case?*

The policeman overheard her and thought she was worried that the criminal would come back. He patted her on the shoulder and said, "Don't worry. This was just a routine slash-and-grab. I'm sure whoever did it is long gone by now. You won't have to worry about them again." Kirstin wasn't so sure.

Just then Arthur and Tricia came back. "A black leather jacket and an accordion folder full of old documents are gone," Tricia told the officer.

CHAPTER 8

ON A COLD, COLD TRAIL

They checked all the garbage cans and dumpsters they could find for two blocks in every direction, hoping that the thief had quickly thrown away the folder after finding out that it was full of worthless old documents. But they found nothing.

Then they called Michael and told him what had happened. Tricia turned up the volume on her cell phone so that they could all hear as they huddled around. Arthur and Kirstin apologized for leaving the documents in the car, but Tricia insisted it was her fault, saying, "I picked the parking spot, and I didn't think it would be a problem to leave the folder in the backseat."

"That's OK, sweetheart," Michael said. "These things happen. Anything in there that we needed was microfilmed years ago. I'll have the records department see how much of it they can reconstruct. In the meantime, why don't you two do what you can and not worry about this. It's no big deal, OK?"

"OK," said Arthur and Kirstin, though they still felt a little guilty.

After that, Tricia dropped them off at Connie's condo. They found him sitting on his living room sofa with a notebook computer in his lap and a big, complicated brace covering most of his right leg. After hearing their story, he said, "It sounds like this will be a tough case to crack. That's a cold, cold trail you're trying to follow."

"We know," sighed Kirstin. "We'll see what Michael can give us. Other than that, I guess we'll try the libraries and museums."

"You might want to give the Historical Society a call too," suggested Connie.

"Good idea," said Arthur. He added it to his "to-do" list. "Maybe we'll be able to dig up some leads."

The documents from the Franklin Company records department arrived the next afternoon, but there were only some employment records for two of Fernando Montoya's sons and a speech Ted Franklin gave on the fiftieth anniversary of the founding of the company, in which he praised "the great contribution Fernando Montoya made to our proud company." Old records that happened to mention the former partner of the company's founder just weren't very important from the perspective of the records department, and very few of them had been microfilmed. It looked like whoever had broken into Tricia's car now had the only copies of most of those documents.

Of the other places they tried, only one, a library archive, had anything helpful. They spent four days looking through blurry microfilm images of old newspapers and magazines in the archive's reading room, which smelled like dust and made Kirstin's allergies act up.

Tricia insisted that the case shouldn't ruin their vacation, so she took them out someplace most nights and several afternoons. They spent one evening wandering around the crowded streets and shops of Chinatown. Kirstin bought a giant painted fan to hang on her bedroom wall at home, and Arthur bought a kung fu sword—with an unsharpened blade. Another time, they went to Fisherman's Wharf, and they spent most of another day exploring Monterey.

That Friday, Arthur, Kirstin, and Connie all sat out on Connie's balcony and talked about how the research was going. Connie asked Arthur a question, but he was looking over the side of the balcony and didn't answer. "Arthur?" repeated Connie.

"What? Oh, sorry, Uncle Connie. I was a little distracted; there's a guy and a girl down there who look like they're completely covered in silver paint—clothes, skin, hair, everything." Kirstin immediately got up to take a look. Sure enough, a man in a suit and a woman in a business dress were walking down the street. They looked completely normal except for the fact that they were covered from head to toe in silver paint.

"There must be a costume party or something," commented Arthur.

Connie shook his head and laughed. "No costume party. Those two are usually out at least once a week for an evening stroll. Welcome to San Francisco!" He waited until his niece and nephew were finished watching. "Now, what have you two found?"

"Well, we're finding lots of stories about what happened to the gold," said Arthur.

"Yeah, but they're all different," added Kirstin. "One story says that Fernando was afraid of being robbed, so he buried his gold in the hills before he left. They say he planned to come back for it with more men later, but he died before he got the chance. But a lot of people went up there digging holes, and none of them found it. Other stories say he abandoned his family and took the gold down to Mexico, where he lived like a king."

"And others say he and the gold were both washed overboard during a storm while he was sailing back to San Francisco," added Arthur.

"It would only wash overboard if it was on deck. Why would he keep his gold on deck?" asked Connie. "He'd put it someplace safer, like the ship's strongbox, don't you think?"

"I wondered the same thing," said Arthur. "The people who believe this story seem to think that he didn't trust the ship's captain or the other passengers, so he hid his gold in a trunk that he labeled 'camp supplies' and gave a box of rocks to the captain to put in the safe."

Connie raised his eyebrows. "And he thought that would make it safer? Sounds a little crazy to me."

"Yeah, that's the one thing a lot of the stories seem to agree on," said Kirstin. "They call him 'Mad Montoya.'"

"Have you guys asked Olivia what she thinks?" asked Connie. They shook their heads. "She and I go to the same church; why don't you mention it to her on Sunday?"

Kirstin fiddled with her glass of lemonade. "Wouldn't it be a little weird to ask her if he was crazy? I mean, he was her relative."

"You don't have to ask if he was crazy," said Connie. "Just ask what she knows about him and his gold. If he said something to anyone, it was probably his family."

Arthur tugged his lower lip as he thought. "That's a good idea, Uncle Connie," he said after a moment. "If he told them where the gold was, they would have gone and gotten it a long time ago. But maybe he told them something else that might be a clue. Like if he sent them a telegram saying he would be bringing the gold, then that means he probably didn't bury it up in the hills somewhere.

"I hope she'll be able to tell us something. We still need to check the ship records to see if there's anything about Fernando or his gold. After that, though, we're pretty much out of leads."

"But someone else isn't," commented Kirstin.

"You mean whoever stole that folder?" asked Arthur.

Kirstin nodded. "For all we know, those documents hold the secret to finding Fernando's treasure. Even if it was just a regular burglar who stole them, how do we know he didn't go through them, figure out what they were, and decide to go after the treasure himself?"

"That would explain why we never found the documents," said Arthur. He thought for a moment. "You know, I wonder if that was 'just a regular burglar.' I saw a man on a black motorcycle behind us as we were driving to Pier 39. He parked about half a block from us, and when we were coming out, I saw him putting something into his bike's saddlebags."

"There's nothing particularly suspicious about riding a motorcycle to Pier 39 and buying something while you're there," observed Connie.

"Maybe not," responded Arthur, "but I'm still going to keep an eye out for black motorcycles while we're here."

CHAPTER 9

THE JOURNAL OF THE *ANNA DALEY*

The Maritime Records Repository was an old, low building near the waterfront. It squatted like a stone toad between two shiny new high rises that kept it in the shade for most of the day. Its once-white limestone was now streaked with orange rust stains and darkened with decades of soot and smog.

Arthur and Kirstin stood on the sidewalk looking doubtfully at the building. "Well, this shouldn't take too long," said Arthur hopefully. This place looked like even less fun than that musty old library archive.

They went through a drab little lobby to a room that said "Clerk" in peeling gold letters over the door. Inside, an old man with a leathery face and scars on his hands sat behind a wide wooden counter. Behind him, shelves of old files filled the room from ceiling to floor. The whole room smelled old and dusty, and Kirstin wished there were some windows open. The man looked up from the crossword puzzle he was working on. "Well, what can I do for you?"

"Do you have any records on the *Anna Daley*?" Arthur asked as they walked up to the counter. The *Anna Daley* was the ship

Ted Franklin (and hopefully Fernando Montoya) had taken on his trip back from the gold fields.

A large book titled "Registry of California Vessel Names: 1800–1995" stood on the counter, but the old man didn't look at it. He wrinkled his forehead and murmured, "*Anna Daley* . . . *Anna Daley*" as he rummaged through the attic of his memory. After a few seconds he looked up. "Coastal and river boat, around the middle of the 1800s, then landfilled, is that the ship you're looking for?"

"Yeah," said Arthur, impressed. "You've got a pretty good memory."

The wrinkles on the man's face piled up at the corners of his mouth as he smiled. "I know pretty much every ship that's ever sailed out the Golden Gate. I've been around ships all my life. I sailed on 'em for forty-two years before I took this job. Why, by the time I was your age, I'd been to Tahiti and China. Have you ever been there?" Arthur hadn't. "Well, make sure you go to the market in Shanghai. You can buy *anything* there, and dirt cheap too. But keep your eye out for thieves. The last time I was there, this huge fellah tried to take my wallet, but I—"

The stuffy air was beginning to make Kirstin's head ache. "I'm sorry," she interrupted, "but we're in a little bit of a hurry." She didn't mention that her main hurry was to get out of the building.

"What? Oh, of course. I'll go on forever if no one stops me. What ship was it that you wanted, young lady?"

"The *Anna Daley.*"

"We won't have any records on her. She's too old. Her log book should be back in the Crypt though. It's right through that door and down the stairs." He pointed to a door with a loose steel knob and chipped green paint.

"The Crypt?" asked Arthur.

The old man nodded. "Those log books are all that's left of a lot of those old ships. Everything they ever did is written down in 'em. The fellah who worked here before me said that they're sort of like the urns that hold people's ashes when they're cremated. So he started calling the room where we keep 'em all 'the Crypt.' You go in there at night, you can just feel the ghosts of all those ships crowding around you." He shivered for emphasis.

"It's a good thing we came during the day then," said Kirstin with a smile.

The old man smiled back. "Sure is. If you'd come at night, the doors would be locked!" He chuckled at his joke as Arthur and Kirstin went into the Crypt.

The ceiling of the Crypt was low and its walls were narrow, but it was very long, making it almost a hallway rather than a room. It was dimly lit by windows in one wall, several of which were partially blocked by huge steel beams that were installed during an earthquake retrofitting project. The wall to their left was filled with very old books, and the wall on their right held newer (but not new) books, with several empty shelves near the door. It was very quiet.

Arthur and Kirstin quickly figured out that the books were organized by date, with the oldest books on their left, beginning at the door. These were in flowing handwritten Spanish that was unreadable even to Arthur, who was getting good grades in Spanish. Fortunately, these books were all too old to have anything to do with the *Anna Daley*.

The detectives slowly walked down rows of dusty books, trying to make out the ship names carved, printed, or written on their ancient leather spines. Every few rows, they would pull out one of the books and check the date on it.

After about half an hour, they found the Gold Rush era log books. That was the good news. The bad news was that there were hundreds and hundreds of them all crammed together in no particular order. "Wow," said Kirstin, picturing how many ships there must have been at San Francisco back then, "where did they put all these ships? It must have been like a floating city."

Arthur's sharp eyes finally spotted what they were looking for. "There it is!" he exclaimed triumphantly, pointing to a series of antique books with the faded words "Anna Daley" barely visible on their spines.

"All right!" said Kirstin happily. "There's a few of these. Let's see: 1842–44, 1845–47, 1848–49 . . ." Her voice trailed off. The last log book was missing! There was a gap where it should have been and marks in the dust on the shelf where a book had recently been pulled out.

Ten seconds later, they were back in front of the old clerk's desk. "Come to think of it, there *was* someone in here not too long ago looking for the *Anna Daley*'s books. Folks aren't supposed to take books out of the Crypt, but sometimes they do anyway," he said. He thought for a moment. "It was a young fellah . . . or actually maybe it was a lady. Yep, I think it was a lady."

"What did she look like?" asked Kirstin.

"She was a brunette . . . no, no, a blonde . . . no, wait a minute." He screwed his eyes shut and concentrated. Arthur and Kirstin waited tensely for at least half a minute while he tried to call up the woman's face from his memory. He opened his lively blue eyes and looked first at Kirstin, then at Arthur. He shook his head. "I just can't remember. I've met so many girls in my life that I can't keep 'em straight anymore. Why, one time I met these five Geisha girls in Japan, and I couldn't tell 'em apart even when they were all right in front of me! They all had on the same makeup and kimonos, see, and—"

But Arthur and Kirstin were thanking him and heading for the door.

CHAPTER 10

THE MONTOYAS

After church on Sunday, Ms. Montoya sat down with Arthur and Kirstin at a local coffee shop to talk. They picked a little round table by the window, which had a nice view of the Embarcadero and the piers and boats beyond it. Arthur told her about Tricia's car getting broken into and the mysterious man on the black motorcycle. Then Kirstin described what they had found—and not found—at the Repository. "Well, it wasn't me," Ms. Montoya said when she heard what the clerk had said about a woman looking for the *Anna Daley*'s records. "Have you asked Tricia Franklin?"

"Not yet, but we will," said Kirstin. "Thanks for offering to help us with our case, Ms. Montoya."

"No problem," she responded. "By the way, please call me Olivia. Everybody else does."

"OK, Olivia," said Arthur. "Speaking of our case, we were wondering if you could tell us anything that might help us solve it."

She thought for a moment, then shook her head. "Nothing springs to mind. I don't have a secret treasure map or anything."

"Maybe you could tell us about your great-great-great-grand-father," suggested Kirstin. "What was he like?"

"Well, for one thing, he's sort of the founding father of our family. He was mayor of our town and had the biggest farm in the county before the Mexican-American War. He was also very loving to his family. My great-grandma told me that her mother told her that once when she was little, a wolf howling in the night really scared her. Her dad sat by her bed all night long so that she felt safe enough to sleep.

"A few years later, he had an accident with a piece of farm machinery. He lost his right arm and part of his foot. After that, it hurt him to walk more than a few yards and he couldn't run very well, but he still tried to play ball with his kids."

Kirstin searched for a tactful way to ask why he was called "Mad Montoya," but (a little to her surprise) Arthur beat her to it. "He sounds really impressive. It's too bad the papers didn't put that in their stories. It seems like all they cared about was different ways he might have hidden his gold. I guess they wanted to paint a picture of him as a crazy old prospector."

"Probably," said Olivia. "Maybe he did act a little overprotective about his gold. California was a pretty lawless place back then, particularly for Mexicans."

Kirstin heard a trace of bitterness in her voice. "What do you mean?" she asked cautiously.

Olivia grimaced a little. "That was just after the Mexican-American War. The Anglos had conquered California and were coming in huge crowds from the East to take over the state. The fact that most of it belonged to Mexicans at the time didn't seem to bother them much."

Kirstin and Arthur sat in awkward silence, not quite sure what they should say. Kirstin fiddled with her teabag while Arthur industriously cleaned up the crumbs from his muffin.

Olivia smiled and her face softened. "I'm sorry. I didn't mean to complain to you guys about ancient history. It's just that Fernando Montoya's farm was taken away by some thugs from the East Coast and we were never able to get it back. That's why he had to take a job as a ranch hand in the first place. And they kicked him out as mayor and put an Anglo soldier in his place. That's bothered my family for a long time." She sighed. "Every time I think about it, I get mad all over again. And then I have to forgive all over again too."

"What do you mean?" asked Kirstin.

"Forgiving people isn't something you do just once and then forget about it," explained Olivia, "or at least it isn't for me. When I think back to something bad someone did to me in the past, it's easy to get mad at them again. And if I don't forgive them again, I haven't really forgiven them at all, have I? I mean, if you stay mad at someone and hold a grudge against them, you haven't really forgiven them in your heart. You've just said the words 'I forgive you' without really meaning them."

"Yeah, I guess so," said Arthur. "I'd never really thought of it that way before. That makes sense, I guess." He was silent for a moment. "Maybe things were so bad for Fernando in California that he took his gold down to Mexico."

Olivia's square jaw tightened and her eyes flashed. "And just abandon his family?" she said angrily. "No way! I've seen those stories too, and they're lies. I can tell you right now you don't need to waste your time on that lead!"

Just then Arthur, who was facing the window, froze. A man had just parked a black motorcycle outside, and it was the same make and model as the one Arthur had seen at Pier 39. The rider wore a black helmet with a tinted visor, and when he took it off Arthur recognized him—it was the same man who was packing his saddlebags at the pier after Tricia's car was robbed. He was broad-shouldered, and he had the same thick mustache and powerful arms Arthur remembered. "There he is!" Arthur whispered hoarsely.

"Who?" asked Kirstin and Olivia together.

"Him!" Arthur whispered, nodding toward him as he walked in. "He's the guy with the black motorcycle!"

The man looked around the shop and noticed them. He looked first at Olivia, then his eyes flicked back and forth between Kirstin and Arthur. He nodded casually to Olivia, who nodded back. Then he walked over to the counter, bought some coffee, and walked out.

Arthur, Kirstin, and Olivia all watched silently until the man left the shop. As soon as the door shut behind him, Arthur turned to Olivia and asked, "Do you know him?"

Olivia nodded. "His name is Carlos Montoya. He's my cousin. Or, well, not exactly my cousin; his great-great-great-grandfather was Fernando's brother, but I've always called him my cousin. All the Montoyas have lived in the same area for over a hundred years, and we've always pretty much been one big family."

"Does he work for the Franklin Company?" asked Kirstin.

"He used to," she said hesitantly.

"What happened, if you don't mind my asking," said Arthur.

"That's OK," said Olivia. "Actually, I'm not sure exactly what happened. He said he quit so he could start up his own business and set his own schedule, but I heard rumors at work that he got fired."

"Did the rumors say why he got fired?" asked Kirstin.

Olivia paused. "Yeah, they said it was for stealing from the company."

Arthur nodded thoughtfully. "Any reason why he'd want to steal a bunch of old documents about Fernando?"

"He's family," said Olivia a little shortly. "I'd rather not talk about him stealing, especially when there's no proof."

"Sorry," said Arthur. "Does he know about Fernando's treasure?"

Olivia shrugged. "Sure, we all know about it. Carlos even went looking for it once a few years ago, but I think that was mostly just an excuse for him and a couple of buddies to take time off from work and go camping." Arthur and Kirstin exchanged quick glances. It looked like they weren't the only ones hunting for the lost treasure of Fernando Montoya!

"Have you told anyone about our investigation?" asked Kirstin.

"I . . ." Olivia stopped and her eyes widened. "The day before I met you guys, I was at a family dinner. I mentioned that Michael had me get the records department to pull all the documents mentioning Fernando so he could give them to some detectives he was meeting Monday morning. Carlos wasn't at the dinner, but his brother was!"

CHAPTER 11

THE ROAD TO
THE GOLD FIELDS

Arthur and Kirstin told the police about what Olivia had said, and they sent an officer to interview both her and Carlos. Carlos admitted hearing about Arthur's and Kirstin's investigation, but he denied having the documents. He also let the police search both his motorcycle and his apartment. They found nothing and dropped the investigation.

Arthur and Kirstin weren't convinced that Carlos was innocent, but the only thing they could do now was try to find the treasure before he did. Their best lead was a long magazine article from 1896 titled "Bicycle Tycoon T. Franklin Gives An Account Of His Adventures." The paper was yellow and brittle and the print was barely readable, but they managed to figure out most of it. It was hard work, but it gave them two crucial clues: it told them the general area where Ted and Fernando had found their gold—"Young Ted decided to prospect in a most unlikely location: a hill three miles due east of the old McCoy camp." It also gave them the route Ted had taken home: "He took his treasure by mule to Sacramento, but, fearing Indians and Mexican bandits, he chose water instead of land for the remainder of his voyage."

The detectives decided that the best thing to do would be to retrace Ted's journey from the spot where he found the gold to the docks of San Francisco. If Fernando had gone with him, the gold had disappeared somewhere between those two points. If it was still there, they would try to find it.

Searching on land would be simple enough. Fernando couldn't have carried the gold very far from the old road, and four hundred pounds of gold would register on just about any metal detector unless it was a lot further underground than a one-armed man could bury it. The real problem was how to search the water part of the journey. If the gold had fallen overboard and was somewhere at the bottom of the Sacramento River or the Pacific Ocean, how would they find it? Arthur and Kirstin had been taking scuba lessons (though Kirstin had only recently started), but there was no way they could swim underwater all the way down the river and then through the San Francisco Bay. Besides, the gold probably would be covered by a thick blanket of mud and silt, making it invisible even if they could stay underwater that long.

Neither of them had any bright ideas for how to handle that problem though. They talked about it for over an hour one afternoon, then they talked about it again the next day. Still nothing. Finally, Arthur threw up his hands and said, "Well, let's look on land and hope it's not underwater."

So that's what they did. They rented two metal detectors, packed up their maps and supplies, and headed for the gold fields. Michael and Tricia had a meeting in Sacramento that day, so they offered to drop off Arthur and Kirstin in the area where Theodore and Fernando had found their gold, and pick them up at the end of the day. Arthur rode "shotgun" next to Michael, while Kirstin and Tricia got the back seat.

After a few minutes of chatting, Kirstin asked Tricia, "Say, were you at the Maritime Records Repository recently?"

Tricia glanced over at her with a surprised look. "The what?"

"The Maritime Records Repository," repeated Kirstin. "We were looking for the journal of the *Anna Daley*, but the last volume was gone. The clerk said he thought a woman had been there recently asking for it, and we were wondering if it might be you."

"Nope." She paused. "Have you asked Olivia Montoya?"

Kirstin laughed. "She said to ask you."

"Would you guys mind if I made a quick call on my car phone?" asked Michael from the front seat. Using buttons on the steering wheel, he scrolled through a list of phone numbers that were displayed on a little screen on the dashboard. When he found the one he wanted, he clicked another button.

"That's a neat car phone," commented Arthur as the number dialed.

"Isn't it?" replied Michael with an amused smile. "I love phone toys, in case you hadn't noticed."

The phone rang once, then a woman's voice said, "Freedom Gear Company."

"Hi, this is Michael Franklin. Is Mr. Freedom available?"

Tricia leaned over to Kirstin. "His parents were hippies," she explained in a whisper.

"I was just calling to let you know we may be a few minutes late for our 11:00 meeting," Michael was saying.

Silence. "I thought our meeting was on Tuesday," said a man's voice from the car's speakers.

"It is Tuesday."

More silence. "You know, I worked through the weekend, and I must've lost track of what day it was. I could have sworn it was Monday today. Listen, I'm really sorry about this. You're on your way to Sacramento right now, aren't you?"

"Yes," said Michael flatly.

"Nuts! Can we reset the closing? We'll do it in your offices so you don't have to make another trip out here. You pick the day."

"Give Olivia a call and she'll set it up for us."

"Thanks! And thanks for not blowing up about this. I really screwed up."

"That's OK," said Michael. "These things happen."

After he turned off the phone, Tricia said, "Well, that's irritating. We just blew a whole day for nothing."

Michael shrugged. "If Fred Freedom were more organized, he'd be making money from his company instead of selling it to me. Besides, it'll be fun to spend a day treasure hunting up in the hills. We're taking the church youth group to the capitol next month, and we were thinking of going hiking afterwards. This will give me a chance to check out the lay of the land."

Throughout the two-hour drive, Arthur watched in the rear-view mirror for black motorcycles, but he saw none. *What is Carlos up to?* Arthur wondered.

CHAPTER 12

A HOLE IN THE GROUND

The green fields and brown scrubland of the Central Valley began to give way to rolling hills again, and the detectives could tell they were getting close. Arthur took out a hand-drawn map he had made by comparing descriptions of where Fernando and Ted found their gold to modern maps of the old gold fields. "OK, turn south on Juniper," he said. Then a few minutes later, "OK, now east on Prairie Creek Road. . . . OK, there's the creek. All right, you can stop anywhere along here. It should be a half mile or so behind that ridge. It doesn't look like there are any roads back there, so we'll have to walk from here."

Michael pulled over and parked on a wide patch of sandy yellow dirt by the side of the road. Warehouses and light industrial buildings lined both sides of the street, but behind them the hills rose in steep ranks. They were bare except for dry grass and bushes, their rocky tops silhouetted against the hot blue sky.

They unpacked their gear and headed out. They were all wearing sunglasses, but even so the bright sun made them squint. As soon as they got past the built-up area, Arthur and Kirstin turned on their metal detectors and started walking in slow zigzags along the sides of the path, watching the readouts on the detectors for any signs of buried metal. Tricia and Michael strolled a little ahead of them, chatting and laughing as they walked.

Tall hills soon rose on either side of the path, giving some shade even though it was close to noon. The trail began to rise steeply as it climbed into the uplands.

"This is hard work," panted Kirstin.

"You think this is hard?" said Arthur as he paused to wipe sweat from his face. "Wait till we have to start digging. *That's* hard work." Kirstin poked tentatively at the ground with her shovel; it was as hard as stone. *Great,* she thought.

After climbing for about a third of a mile, the path leveled off and widened out into a small valley enclosed by cliffs of reddish-brown rock. "Look!" said Michael, picking up a rounded pebble. "These rocks are all smooth. That means this must be an old riverbed. It looks like you've led us to Ted and Fernando's claim, Arthur. Nice work!"

"Thanks," said Arthur, surveying the little canyon with excitement. "If Fernando buried his treasure anywhere, it's in here."

"How do you figure that?" asked Tricia.

"Well, he couldn't have carried four hundred pounds of gold very far himself, so he would have had to bury it somewhere he could get to with a horse or donkey. The country around here is pretty rough, so he would have been more or less limited to the road, the path leading up here, and this place. If he had buried it along the road, it would have been discovered when they dug the foundations for all those buildings. And we didn't find it when we searched along the path leading up here, so it must be in here someplace."

Arthur and Kirstin methodically walked up and down the valley with their metal detectors, starting at the riverbed and working out toward the stone walls. Michael and Tricia volunteered to help, but there were only two detectors. Also, hunting for buried treasure was a job the two detectives were perfectly happy to do on their own.

They walked back and forth under the bright, hot sun for about half an hour without finding anything except the skeleton of a goat that had apparently fallen off one of the sheer cliffs that walled in the valley. Then the dial on Arthur's detector suddenly swung up in a sharp spike.

Arthur stopped, his heart pounding. He swept the detector's round head slowly back and forth. There it was again! "I've found something!" he yelled. The others grabbed the digging tools and came running. Arthur looked at the display again and his heart sank. "It doesn't look very big," he said apologetically as Kirstin and the Franklins gathered around him, "and it doesn't look like it's made of gold."

"Well, let's at least dig it up and find out," said Kirstin, handing her brother a shovel. It took twenty minutes of hard work to get less than a foot down. They were both sweating heavily, and Kirstin was about to suggest that they give up, when Arthur's shovel hit something that made a loud "crunch!" They could see a shiny glint at the bottom of the hole.

Arthur and Kirstin dropped their shovels and got down on their hands and knees for a closer look. Shards of glass poked out of the dirt. Mixed in with them were a variety of animal bones and a bent and badly rusted shovel blade, which was what had registered on Arthur's detector.

Arthur carefully worked the various items free from the soil.

Some of the splinters of glass had letters embedded in them, and Kirstin took the pieces as Arthur handed them to her and started fitting them together. She quickly realized they had found the remains of a long-necked bottle that would have held about a quart. With growing excitement, she read the letters embossed in the glass. Across one side were big letters reading "Adelman's Finest Malt Whiskey," but what excited Kirstin were the little letters along the bottom that said, "bottled in S. F. Cal. 1849." Then Arthur found a piece with the letters "F. M." scratched into it. "This is definitely the spot!" he said as he got to his feet and knocked the dirt off his hands.

"It looks like we've found Ted and Fernando's garbage pit," said Michael approvingly as he examined the piece of glass with Fernando's initials.

"Congratulations!" Kirstin said to her brother. "You've found Fernando's trash. Now let's see if we can find his treasure!"

Two hours later, they hadn't found anything more, and they were nearly done searching the valley floor. The sun was starting to slide down the sky, but the valley ran northeast to southwest, so the tall cliffs at its sides didn't offer any shade in the afternoon. The sun stood exactly over the canyon wall that Kirstin was working toward. The stone had looked smooth earlier in the day, but now even the slightest imperfection was picked out by the harsh light shining straight down the cliff face.

Kirstin made her last pass with the metal detector right at the foot of the cliff. She couldn't help looking up at the bizarre, shifting patterns of light and shadow on the stone wall beside her. A small lizard ran along the cliff face, casting a ten-foot-long shadow that pointed at it like an arrow. A depression a quarter of an inch deep—invisible the rest of the day—was a pool of shade on the brightly lit rock.

Then Kirstin noticed something at eye level right beside her: someone had carved "TIF" in three-foot-high letters in the stone. The carving was very faint and looked old and weathered, which she guessed was why they hadn't noticed it earlier. But now the letters were filled with shadow and she could see them clearly. She stepped back for a better view. She could see that the line between the T and the F was too long to be the letter I. Was this how Ted and Fernando had marked their claim: "T/F"? Or had Ted cut his initials in the wall the same way Fernando marked his whiskey bottle? But why would he do that? And why would he put a big line between his first and last initials?

Kirstin opened her mouth to call out to the others, but just then Tricia yelled from the opposite side of the canyon, "Kirstin! Hey Kirstin, come over here!" Kirstin put down her metal detector and jogged over. Bright late afternoon sun and dark shadows streaked the dry riverbed between her and Tricia, making it difficult for Kirstin to see the little ridge of dried mud in front of her. And she never saw the deep hole behind the ridge.

When Kirstin was about twenty yards from Tricia, she suddenly lost her footing and found herself falling in darkness. She screamed, but her voice was cut off when she landed with crushing force.

CHAPTER 13

BEATING CARLOS

Kirstin must have blacked out when she landed, because the next thing she remembered was being hit in the face by sand and little pebbles as Arthur tried to climb down to her. "Hold on a sec!" she protested weakly. "You're knocking stuff onto my face!"

The shower of debris stopped immediately. "Kirstin, are you OK?" called Arthur in a relieved voice. "Why didn't you say anything when we yelled down to you? We were really scared!"

"Yeah, I think I'm all right," said Kirstin as she sat up and gingerly checked her body. She was sore and covered in cold mud, but otherwise she was OK. She carefully got to her feet and found that she was standing in several inches of sticky mud. She looked up at the circle of light about five feet above her head. She could see three heads silhouetted around its edge. "The fall must have knocked me out. How did I get down here? And where did all this mud come from?"

"You fell into a sinkhole," explained Michael. "The river-bed may be dry, but often there's still water underground. Sometimes it makes a hole in the surface like this one."

"I saw it when I was going back and forth with my metal

detector," said Arthur, "but I didn't know what it was. I should've said something."

"And I shouldn't have made you run across the canyon like that," said Tricia. "I noticed you looking at those shadows on the wall, and I wanted you to see the view from over here, which was really great. I knew it wouldn't last for more than a few minutes, so I yelled to you. Big mistake. I'm glad you're OK."

"Me too," said Kirstin. She reached for a handhold in the dirt walls of the hole, but the underground soil was moist and soft. "I don't think I can climb out of here," she said. "Could you guys give me a hand?"

They reached down to her with a shovel, which she grabbed and held onto tightly as they pulled her out. She stood on the valley floor again, covered in half-dry brown mud. The sun had disappeared below the end of the valley, but the heat of the day still rose from the rocks and hard dirt of the canyon. It felt good on her chilled and bruised arms and legs.

They helped her down to the car, where she scraped off as much of the mud as she could. Exhausted, she got in, relaxed into the soft seats, turned the cool breeze of the air conditioning on her face, and waited for Arthur and Michael to finish packing their equipment into the trunk. By the time they were done two minutes later, she was fast asleep.

Connie's balcony had a beautiful moonlit view of the fog coming in through the Golden Gate, the gap between San Francisco and the Marin Headlands that allowed ships to sail between the Pacific Ocean and the San Francisco Bay. The graceful spans of the Golden Gate Bridge rose out of the fog like trees in a field of new snow. Arthur and Kirstin held cups of hot chocolate and sat looking out at the peaceful scene. Connie was sitting in a chair across from them with his leg up, listening to them tell about the day's events. "So the doctor said I might have had a mild concussion, but that I should be fine as long as I don't bang my head against anything for a few weeks," concluded Kirstin.

"Sounds like good advice," commented Connie. "And I say we stay out of the gold fields for a while. It seems like every time we go there, someone winds up in the hospital."

"I don't think we'll have much reason to go back there," said Arthur. "It's a pretty safe bet that Fernando's treasure isn't there."

Kirstin nodded. "We looked everywhere it could be."

"And you know what else we didn't find up there?" said Arthur. "Any sign of Carlos. No black motorcycle behind us on the highway, no footprints or tire tracks up in the canyon, nothing."

"Did you expect to see him?" asked Connie.

"I thought we might," answered Arthur. "Olivia said he'd gone treasure hunting up in that general area once before, but now that he's got our documents and that logbook—or we think he does anyway—"

"I thought the man at the Repository said a *woman* took the logbook," interjected Kirstin.

"He said he *thought* it was a woman, but he wasn't sure," corrected Arthur. "Besides, I got the impression that he remembers ships a lot better than he remembers people.

Anyway, now I think that Carlos knew the gold wasn't up there and didn't bother looking. My guess is that he figured out something from those papers he stole that told him that the gold made it onto the *Anna Daley*. That would explain why he wouldn't bother searching on land. It also explains why he would want the *Anna Daley*'s logbook and wouldn't want us to have it."

"But why would Carlos be trying to beat you to the treasure in the first place?" asked Connie. "Isn't he a Montoya?"

"Yeah," said Kirstin, "but he's not descended from Fernando, so he wouldn't get any gold we find, would he?"

Connie shook his head. "I'm not an expert on California's inheritance laws, but I don't think he would." He thought for a moment. "OK, what's your plan for beating Carlos?"

"Well, if the gold was on the *Anna Daley*, but didn't make it to San Francisco, then it's probably somewhere on the bottom of the Sacramento River or the Bay," answered Arthur. "We'll search there."

"And how are you going to do that?"

Arthur hesitated. "That's the hard part," he admitted.

CHAPTER 14

SHADOWS IN THE SEA

Arthur, Kirstin, Michael, Tricia, and Olivia all sat around the steel and glass table in Michael's office. "So you need some underwater metal detecting equipment?" Michael asked. Arthur and Kirstin both nodded. "OK. One of my fraternity brothers is in the marine salvage business. I'll bet he could help. Hold on a second." He paused. "Edward Hofsacker," he said in a loud, clear voice. Arthur and Kirstin sat in surprised silence. Maybe this would be easier than they had thought.

"Crazy Eddie?" interjected Tricia.

"Shhhhhh," said Michael. "It's ringing."

A second later, a man's voice with a strong Texas twang said, "Hello, Ed Hofsacker here."

"Hi, it's Mike Franklin. I've got Tricia, Olivia, and a couple of detectives here with me."

"Now Mike, what're the detectives for? What're you investigatin'? If you're still tryin' to find out who shaved your head while you were asleep that one time, I can tell you right now I had nothin' to do with that. Well, not much anyway."

Michael laughed. "I still think you're the one who fed me the knockout drops so I wouldn't wake up, but that's not what they're investigating. Actually, we're looking for lost treasure from the Gold Rush."

Ed gave a long whistle. "Lost treasure, huh? Wish I could be there for that. Oh well. So, what can I do for y'all?"

"Well, it looks like the gold might be at the bottom of the Bay or the Sacramento River. I was wondering whether you might have any underwater metal detecting equipment we could rent."

"Metal detectors? Hold on, lemme check my equipment inventory." Ed was silent for a minute and they could hear computer keys clicking in the background. "No, I don't have any metal detectors you can rent." Arthur's and Kirstin's hearts sank. "But I do have one y'all can borrow."

They all laughed. "Thanks, Ed. I owe you one," said Michael gratefully. "How about some shark fishing on my new boat? Just let me know the next time you'll be out this way."

"Sounds like a fair deal. I'll have that equipment shipped to y'all today. You should have it by day after tomorrow."

Two mornings later, Arthur carefully piloted Michael's boat out of the marina. It had a cabin and was bigger than any other boat he had operated. He recognized most of the controls, though, and it handled well. Kirstin's head popped out of the cabin. "How's it going, Arthur?" she asked.

"Just fine. This is a lot easier than the last time I learned to pilot a new boat," he said with a grin. They had been on the trail of the Autumn Rose; a gang of Vietnamese thugs had been shooting at Arthur and had hit the boat's gas line. He barely had time to jump in the water before the boat had exploded and sunk.

"When was that?" asked Kirstin. Then she remembered and smiled too. "Oh yeah. Well, try to return this boat in one piece," she said as she ducked back into the cabin.

It was a bright, hot day, but Arthur had a couple of sweatshirts and windbreakers on the seat next to him. It was warm enough now, but if the fog came in, it could get cold and wet fast. Also, their search would probably take them all the way across the Bay, and they would want something warm to wear in the boat if they had to go diving in the cold waters of the Pacific Ocean.

Olivia sat in the back of the boat watching the monitor's display. To Arthur, it looked like just a bunch of squiggly lines. But Olivia and Kirstin had spent an hour and a half with a technician learning how to read it while Arthur learned about the boat. To them, it showed any piece of metal that weighed more than fifty or sixty pounds. It also had magnetic sensors that showed whether the metal contained any iron. There was only room for one person at the monitor, so Kirstin sat on the deck enjoying the sun while she waited for her turn to watch.

They took the boat up to where Fernando Montoya's last journey would have started and retraced his voyage. He would have gotten on board at Sacramento, then traveled down the Sacramento River to the San Francisco Bay. His ship would have crossed the Bay, then sailed along the shoreline and docked at the old port area on the northern coast of San Francisco.

The first few hours of their search were pretty uneventful. Olivia stopped them twice after spotting things on the metal detector. The first time, it was a sunken aluminum boat in the Sacramento River. The second time, they found a half-buried length of lead pipe sticking out of the bottom of the Bay.

"Hey, what's that?" asked Kirstin nervously as they made their way through the open Bay. Arthur and Olivia turned and saw something large and gray slipping beneath the waves.

"Looks like a shark," answered Arthur. "They should be big and hungry this time of year, but they only eat fish and sea lions. They usually only attack humans by mistake, like when people are thrashing around in the surf and all the motion gets the shark excited."

"So if you get in the water, don't do anything exciting," Olivia suggested with a laugh.

They didn't see any more sharks as they slowly made their way along the San Francisco shoreline, but Kirstin (who was now watching the monitors) did notice a couple of suspicious shadows on the sonar display. She hadn't been paying much attention to the sonar because it wouldn't show them buried gold and therefore wasn't much help in their treasure hunt. What the sonar did show, though, was any objects between the bottom of their boat and the sea floor. There were lots of these. Kirstin could make out schools of fish, boulders on the bottom, and even a sunken ship.

In fact, she was watching the sonar screen so closely that she didn't notice that the metal detector was going crazy. As she was trying to make out what looked like another shark on the sonar, the line on the metal detector went way up. It reached a sharp peak while she was watching a school of fish and had almost fallen back to normal when she spotted the shipwreck. "Hey, check this out," Kirstin called to the other two as the shipwreck came into full view on the sonar monitor.

Arthur shut down the engine, and he and Olivia made their way back to Kirstin. She was about to point out the shipwreck when Olivia said, "Wow! This is the biggest one yet!" She was looking at the paper strip that came out of the metal detector and recorded all of its findings. "Nice going, Kirstin!"

"Uh, thanks," said Kirstin a little sheepishly.

"Let's get our gear on," said Arthur, reaching for his diving equipment.

"Can't you go by yourself this time?" asked Kirstin. "I'm feeling a little sick."

Arthur stopped. "I'm not certified to dive solo. You know that."

"Yeah, but you've been diving for over a year now. Besides, this is simple diving; you just go straight down, see what's on the bottom, and come straight back up."

"Kirstin, this could be *it*!" Arthur said in frustration. "Don't you want to go?"

"Sure," she replied, "but I feel sick to my stomach, so I shouldn't be diving." She did feel a little sick. She also didn't particularly want to put on her wetsuit and get into the chilly water again, but she didn't mention that.

Arthur knew that if she really was sick to her stomach, she shouldn't dive (throwing up into your mouthpiece is dangerous as well as gross), but he also knew that his sister was not a big fan of doing anything uncomfortable. "Are you *sure* you're sick?" he asked suspiciously.

"Uh-huh," she nodded.

"Well, OK—but next time you're either going with me or we're calling it a day."

"Deal," she said with relief. "Thanks!"

Arthur took a "bang stick" in addition to his standard diving gear. A bang stick's name pretty well describes what it is, a stick about three feet long with a handle on one end and a little bomb on the other. A diver who will be swimming with sharks often brings a bang stick to push away sharks that get too close for comfort. If the shark won't take the hint, the diver can jab hard with the bang stick, which will make the bomb go off. Arthur didn't know if the big sharks of San Francisco Bay (ten-foot-long Broadnose Sevengills) had ever attacked humans in the wild, but he had read about them going after divers in aquariums.

He also took a reel and line in case he had to do any wreck diving. The shipwreck Kirstin had spotted almost certainly wasn't the *Anna Daley*—a 150-year-old wreck would be too decayed to show up on sonar like that—but whatever had set off the metal detector might be on board the wreck or under it. Besides, he had earned his wreck diving certification earlier in the summer and enjoyed using it whenever possible.

Arthur climbed down the boat's ladder and started swimming for the bottom. The bright white-yellow sunlight vanished as he went under and was replaced by the cool greenish blue of the sea. He started kicking toward the bottom, looking for whatever they had seen on the metal detector.

A shadow passed over him and he looked up. He saw a large shape swimming with lazy strength through the water above him. Yup, there were sharks here. He checked the bang stick and kept swimming for the bottom.

The light dimmed as he went deeper, so he turned on his diving light. He soon saw the brown mud bottom ahead, but he didn't see whatever had shown up on the monitor. He turned on his portable metal detector, and it started to ping faintly. He swam in a slow circle until it got louder, then followed it as the signal got stronger and stronger.

The pinging got so loud that he had to turn the volume down. Then his light caught a glint of metal ahead. He swam toward it eagerly, not needing the metal detector anymore.

Arthur reached the shiny object and saw what it was: a bright metal fin attached to the top of a dull gray teardrop-shaped object. It looked like a bomb, but based on the metal detector's signal, this thing was solid metal, probably lead. There was no rust, weeds, or silt on it anywhere, so it must have been on the bottom for only a very short time. It seemed almost as if someone had put it there just so it would set off their metal detector, but why would anyone want to do that?

CHAPTER 15

FRENZY!

Back on the surface, the fog rolled in. It began with gauzy streamers reaching for shore like ghostly tentacles. Then a thick white wall marched over the small waves and engulfed the boat. Within five minutes, Kirstin couldn't see one end of the boat from the other. They were only about a quarter of a mile from shore, but it felt like they were completely alone in a sea of cold mist. "Better turn on the lights," Olivia's voice called out of the fog. "We wouldn't want anyone to run us down."

Kirstin switched on the lights, but all they seemed to do was make short cones of glowing mist that ended less than ten feet from the sides of the boat. She shivered and put on her sweatshirt and windbreaker; the fog wasn't just thick, it was cold and wet.

Suddenly they heard the sound of a motorboat approaching. As the sound got close—dangerously close—Kirstin began to worry that the boat would run over Arthur if he came up, which he might at any moment. They had raised a flag with the "diver down" symbol, of course, but the people on the other boat probably couldn't see it in the fog. "Hey! Diver down! Diver down!" Kirstin yelled into the mist.

The other boat slowed down, but didn't seem to be going

away. Kirstin let out a blast from the boat's air horn. "Hey! We've got a diver down!" she yelled at the top of her lungs.

"You have to leave this area!" Olivia yelled.

Still no response. The other boat seemed to be making slow passes back and forth just where Arthur was diving. Kirstin had once seen a manatee that had been run over by a motorboat, and she vividly remembered the deep gouges that the propeller blades had made in the animal's back. She was trying very hard not to picture what would happen if Arthur got hit.

She prayed fervently for her brother as she and Olivia yelled frantically and blasted the horn. But the other boat just ignored them. "What are they doing?" Kirstin asked in frustration. Just then, they caught a glimpse of the other boat at the very edge of one of the cones of light cast by their running lights. It was hard to make out, but someone appeared to be dumping something over the side.

Olivia was just calling the Coast Guard when the other boat suddenly revved its engine and sped away.

"Whew!" said Kirstin with relief. "Thank God that Arthur didn't come up yet. Those idiots could have killed him!"

Olivia shook her head. "I wonder what they were doing. They didn't seem to be fishing, and it's too foggy for water skiing or sightseeing."

"Speaking of sightseeing, I wonder what Arthur is doing down there," said Kirstin. "This has already taken twice as long as our first two dives." She looked over the side and something caught her eye: the water looked funny for some reason.

"Maybe we can spot him on the sonar," said Olivia as she walked over to the monitor.

"Sounds good," said Kirstin. "I'm just going to check

something out here." She turned one of the lights so that it pointed straight down. The water had been greenish gray, but now it was a murky red-brown. She scooped some up in her hand for a better look. There was definitely something in it, but what? Kirstin sniffed it gingerly. It had a familiar iron smell that she couldn't place right away. "It smells like . . . like . . ." she muttered to herself. Then it hit her: *blood*.

She stood frozen for a second as the bloody water slipped through her fingers and made a little rust-colored pool on the deck. Then she grabbed the spotlight and frantically swept its beam across the dark water, looking for (but afraid to see) what was left of her brother after the propeller had mangled him.

A second later she realized with relief that it couldn't be Arthur's blood; there was too much of it. The dark stain spread across the water as far as she could see in the murk. A new chill ran down her spine as she remembered the mystery boat pouring something into the water. Why would they dump gallons and gallons of blood into the ocean?

Something big splashed in the fog. Kirstin swung the light over toward it. She saw ripples and a big swirl, as if a huge fish was thrashing just below the surface. Just then Olivia called to her, "Kirstin, look at this!"

Something in her voice made Kirstin run, not walk, over to the monitor. The screen showed a dozen large teardrop shapes twisting and darting wildly around the screen. "Sharks," said Olivia, her voice shaking. "Something down there is making them crazy."

Kirstin gasped as she realized what was happening. "No, something up here. That other boat dumped tons of blood in the water. They knew Arthur was down there and filled the water with blood so the sharks would go into a feeding frenzy!"

CHAPTER 16

SHIPWRECK

Arthur backed away from the lead object and headed for the surface. After going just a few feet, though, he stopped. A dark cloud filled the water above him and was slowly sinking. He treaded water for a moment, unsure whether to try swimming through the cloud or look for a way around it. *What is it anyway?* he wondered.

Suddenly a dark shape shot out of the cloud and straight at him. He had no time to react before it slammed into him, knocking him backward and giving his arm a terrible yank as it dragged him toward the bottom. Then he found himself floating again, and his right arm throbbed with pain. He looked down and saw why: the shark (he realized that was what had attacked him) had grabbed his diving light in its jaws and pulled him with it until the wrist strap had snapped. He moved his wrist gingerly but couldn't tell whether it was broken.

He glanced up and saw the shark coming back. He looked around frantically for someplace to hide. He saw a large and promising-looking shadow on the ocean floor to his left, but that was at least twenty yards away; there was no way he could reach it before the shark reached him.

He clutched his bang stick in his good hand and crouched

on the bottom, feeling very vulnerable. The shark started to circle Arthur, as if wondering if any part of him tasted better than the diving light. As soon as he saw that it wasn't going to attack immediately, he started moving warily toward the shadow.

He was in the middle of asking God to save him from the shark when two more streaked out of the dark cloud and started toward him. The first shark didn't want to lose its meal to the newcomers, so it broke off its circle and sped straight at him. Now instead of one shark, he had three to deal with!

He pointed the bang stick at the closest shark and braced for the impact. The shark opened its jaws wide as it came close, its rows of jagged teeth reaching out for Arthur's arm. He aimed for its nose, but it aimed for his hand. He yelled as he saw the bang stick and his hand both disappear inside its wide-open mouth.

As the shark's jaws closed on his arm, Arthur felt a jolt and heard a muffled "thump!" as the explosive on his bang stick went off. The shark let go of his arm and began thrashing wildly. A dark red mist leaked from its mouth.

Arthur kicked away from the injured shark just in time. The other two sharks hit it like battering rams, tearing huge mouthfuls out of its sides. In a few seconds, the water was full of shark blood and other sharks were coming to join the feast.

Arthur dropped the remains of his bang stick and swam for the shipwreck as fast as he could. His left arm stung fiercely, and he glanced at it as he swam. The shark's teeth had shredded his wetsuit sleeve and left a long cut on his forearm. He could see the blood leaking from it and drifting away through the water. *Perfect for attracting more sharks*, he thought grimly.

He was right. The injured shark was gone now, and the other sharks were starting to scatter. Two of them swam in his direction. He swam as fast as he could for cover, doing his best to ignore the pain shooting through both arms.

The shadow loomed in front of him and took shape in the watery half-light: a shipwreck. It lay on its side, the bottom of its rusty, weed-covered hull facing him. He looked desperately for a hole he could duck into, but saw none. He glanced back and wished he hadn't—the sharks were definitely following him, and they were only a few yards away.

Arthur swam up over the hull, searching for a window or door in the murky darkness. There! A porthole, its glass long gone, opened ahead of him. He couldn't see what lay inside, but he didn't much care. He grabbed the edge and pulled himself inside. He heard a noise behind him and turned to see the bigger of the sharks struggling to get its nose free from the porthole. After a second, it got itself loose and swam away. That had been close!

He breathed a sigh of relief, said a silent prayer of thanks, and looked around. He was in a long hallway that appeared to run all the way along the side of the wreck, punctuated every ten feet or so by portholes. It was tough to see much of anything though, because there was so little light and the hall was half-full of silt. The only sounds were the soft hiss of the ocean currents and occasional clanks and groans from the dead ship.

He took the little secondary light off of his belt and turned it on, but its beam was basically useless in the cloudy water. He decided to swim down the hallway, then look for a way to get out of the ship at the other end—away from the sharks. He would have to be very careful though, because the visibility was low and shipwrecks are full of unstable walls and jags of metal and glass just waiting to crush a diver or tear his air hoses. He also didn't have a buddy who could help him if he got in trouble, which could happen very easily inside a shipwreck.

He clipped his line onto a bolt sticking out from a bulkhead and made sure it was coming out of the reel smoothly. If his plan worked and he emerged from the far end of the wreck, he'd simply drop the reel and head for the surface. But if he got lost or his path was blocked, he'd want to have the line so that he could find his way back out.

A movement caught his eye, and he turned to see a shark squeezing through the porthole he had come through. It was the smaller of the two that had chased him into the wreck, but it was still much bigger than he was. He kicked off the wall and swam as fast as he dared down the hallway.

Arthur stirred up quite a bit of silt as he swam, and he hoped that would hide him from the shark. He ducked down another passage that was even darker than the first one. He stopped after a few yards and hung motionless in the shadowy water, waiting to see whether the shark would swim past and miss him.

He held his breath as a long torpedo-shaped silhouette swam by above, paused for a moment, then turned into the passage he had taken. He turned and fled down into the darkness.

The jagged end of a torn steel beam appeared just in front of him. He barely managed to duck to the side in time to avoid impaling himself on it, but he crashed into a pile of mud and waterlogged wood instead. He looked around frantically for a way past the obstruction, but found none; the rest of the hall he had chosen was clogged with debris.

Trapped! Arthur looked back at the shark. The cloud of mud and wood fragments he had created confused it momentarily, but now it was coming toward him again. In desperation, he decided to try to swim past the shark at top speed and hope that its teeth missed him. He put his hand on the wall to brace himself and found something he had missed before: a door handle. He yanked at it and, to his surprise, it opened easily.

He swam in and tried to pull the door shut behind him, but the inside handle broke off in his hand. The place where he found himself was completely black, like the inside of a closet on a starless midnight. Arthur swam to his left, one hand trailing along the wall and the other in front of him so he wouldn't run into some unseen obstacle. He reached the far wall of the room, which was very big, and turned to see the shark coming through the door behind him.

The shark was between him and the only door, and he had no idea how he could get past it. He had been half-thinking that he was smarter than the shark and would somehow figure out a way to beat it. Then he realized that the shark didn't *need* to be smarter than he was; if he tried to escape, it could easily outswim him. If he tried to hide, it could smell his blood and sense his smallest movement, even in total darkness. In a few seconds the shark would reach him, and there was nothing he could do to escape. He couldn't help imagining what it would feel like as those tooth-filled jaws clamped down on him, tearing through his wetsuit and skin and crunching into his bones. Fear clouded his mind, and he could feel himself starting to panic.

CHAPTER 17

AIR

A rthur took a deep breath, and that gave him a desperate idea. Sharks are drawn to erratic motion, so if he could create some, maybe he would have a chance to reach the door while the shark was distracted. He just might have figured out a way to create *a lot* of erratic motion, but it would mean getting rid of his air tank. That would leave him with only his emergency bottle of "spare air," and he wasn't at all sure that it would be enough to get him to the surface. The ship was thirty or forty feet underwater, and he was way down inside it. He didn't have much choice though; if he didn't do something *now*, the shark would start ripping him into bite-size pieces.

He took a couple more deep breaths as fast as he could while he took off his air tank. He held the last breath, spat out the mouthpiece, and jammed the top of the tank into a crack in the wall. Then he squeezed himself into the corner for leverage and kicked the tank as hard as he could with both feet. The regulator at the top of the tank broke off and the tank shot away like a rocket as the compressed air inside jetted out through the hole. It thundered past the shark, smashed into the far wall of the room with a tremendous BOOM! and zipped off in another direction. The shark turned in a flash and swam after it.

A loud groan rumbled through the dead ship, and Arthur saw the faint outline of the door move and then disappear in a swirl of silt. He realized that the wreck must be unstable and that the impact of his tank on the wall had caused it to shift on the sea bottom.

Arthur pushed off the wall and swam as fast as he could through the cloudy water toward where he thought the door was. He hoped he could find it before the air in the tank ran out and the shark turned its attention back to him.

He was still about twenty feet away when the last of the air dribbled out and the tank fell into silt at the bottom of the room with a soft thud. The shark swam over and nosed it, but almost immediately abandoned it and swam toward Arthur. He couldn't see his hunter clearly in the gloom, but he caught glimpses of its swift movements as it swam to cut him off. He tried not to look at it.

The door was ten feet away! Now five feet! Something grabbed his left flipper, pulling it off his foot. Now he was through the doorway! He seized the door and slammed it shut. The shark pushed on the door from inside, and it started to open! Arthur braced his feet on a metal beam and pushed the door shut with all his might. He slid the latch into place, locking his enemy inside.

He desperately needed to breathe. His air tank was gone, of course, so he pulled out his little emergency air bottle and took a deep breath. He wanted to take more, but he couldn't— the emergency bottle would only last for a few minutes, and he would need all of that time if he was going to have any hope of reaching the surface alive.

And getting out of the ship alive would be awfully hard without his reel and line—which he discovered he no longer had. He must have dropped the reel while he was trying to escape from the shark. He felt around for it blindly in the mud and debris beneath him for what seemed like hours. Finally he found the line and traced it down to the reel.

Arthur dropped his diving weights, hooked his left foot behind his right, and dolphin-kicked straight up with his one remaining flipper, swimming back up the cloudy hall as fast as he could. The line should take him back to the long hallway with the portholes. If he could find a porthole fast and if it was open, he might be able to reach the surface before his air ran out. Or he might not.

He knew his air must be almost gone, and he wondered if he could make it even if there was an open porthole somewhere above him. Maybe he had escaped one death just to die another.

"Are there any more of those bang sticks?" Kirstin asked as she struggled with the air tank. Olivia had called the Coast Guard, but it would be at least another fifteen minutes before a cutter could reach them. That was fifteen minutes Arthur didn't have, so Kirstin was getting ready to go down and help her brother. She guiltily thought of him down there by himself and wondered what was happening.

"No," Olivia answered, "but I did find a club for stunning fish. You want that?"

"It'll have to do," Kirstin answered as she strapped the tank onto her back. She pulled the mask down over her eyes and nose and bit the mouthpiece of the air hose. Olivia turned the knob on the tank and Kirstin heard the metallic hiss of air coming into the hose. It was time. She took a deep breath and started down the ladder on the side of the boat.

She was in the water to her knees when her cell phone rang. She jumped and nearly lost her grip on the ladder. Olivia held it out to her. "Do you want to answer it?"

Kirstin hesitated, but decided to see who it was. She took the phone from Olivia. "Hello?"

"Hi, Kirstin," said Arthur. "You won't believe what just happened to me!"

She stood stunned for several seconds. "You're right. Are you OK? Where are you?"

"I'm at a payphone on Pier 39," he answered. "I think my right wrist is sprained and I've got a big cut on my left arm, but other than that I'm OK."

"It is so great to hear from you! We thought you were shark food!" Kirstin covered the mouthpiece. "He's on Pier 39 and he's OK!" she called to Olivia, who was watching the sonar. "So what happened?" Kirstin said into the phone.

"I can't give you all the details right now because there's a policeman here who really wants to talk to me and the paramedics need to get me on oxygen so I don't get decompression sickness. But here's the short version: there were sharks all over down there, and I just barely got away from them. I had to ditch my air tank, and I nearly drowned before I reached the surface. It was all foggy when I came up, and I couldn't see you guys. I did see these lights though, so I swam toward them. Turns out it was the lights on Pier 39—I was only about a hundred yards from the end of the pier. So here I am."

"Wow!" exclaimed Kirstin. "OK, we'll take the boat over

and find a spot to tie it up. We'll meet you there in a few minutes."

She turned off the phone and climbed back into the boat, her relief rapidly turning to anger and fear. Someone—she had a pretty good idea who—had just tried to kill Arthur, and possibly her too. *This isn't just about finding a treasure anymore*, Kirstin promised herself grimly. *It's about putting Carlos Montoya behind bars!*

CHAPTER 18

THANK YOU VERY, VERY MUCH!

Michael Franklin raised his glass and said, "I'd just like to thank Arthur and Kirstin Davis for their outstanding work on this case. You two did everything I expected and more. You dug up every clue that was out there, you found every important document, and you even did a full search for the treasure. You managed to do all this despite losing your guide and chauffeur to a knee injury," here he nodded to Connie, who chuckled, "despite losing your case file to a car burglar, and despite Arthur being the victim of what looks like a very sick crime.

"You didn't bring us Fernando Montoya's treasure, but you did bring us something almost as good: closure. We can now put to rest those stories that Fernando's treasure is still somewhere out there in the hills. And we can safely say that we—or rather you—have done everything that can be done to find out what happened to him and to his gold. I think I speak for everyone here and for many who aren't here when I say thank you very, very much!"

Olivia, Tricia, and Connie smiled and raised their glasses too, joining Michael in toasting the two detectives. "Yes, thanks," said Olivia.

"You two did a great job!" added Tricia.

"Thanks," said Arthur without much enthusiasm.

Kirstin nodded and gave a small smile. "It was nothing," she said, and she meant it.

They were all sitting around a table in a small private dining room in one of San Francisco's best restaurants, situated on top of one of its tallest buildings. The view from the floor to ceiling windows was spectacular and the food was even better, but Arthur and Kirstin weren't enjoying either.

As soon as Michael had heard what happened off Pier 39, he had paid Arthur and Kirstin for their work and declared the case closed. He was very nice about it, and he had arranged this dinner to thank them, but they were still disappointed and frustrated. Whatever Michael might say, they knew in their hearts that the Davis Detective Agency had failed to solve a case for the very first time.

Worse, Carlos had probably managed to beat them. The police had taken him in for questioning and searched his apartment again, of course. They had also investigated all businesses in the Bay Area that dealt with animal or human blood. They had even checked with anybody in San Francisco who sold or rented boats to see if they had done business with Carlos recently.

The police hadn't found anything, and Arthur and Kirstin doubted they would. Carlos had shown an uncanny ability to guess his opponents' moves, and there was no reason to think he couldn't do it now. He had gotten rid of any incriminating evidence before the police had investigated him last time, and he'd probably done it this time too. The police would likely keep an eye on him for a while, then give up when he didn't do anything else suspicious. After that, he could continue his treasure hunt without having to worry about any teenage detectives. That *really* irritated Arthur and Kirstin. There wasn't much they could do about it that night, though, so they gritted their teeth and did their best to be polite guests of honor.

The next morning, Kirstin, Arthur, and Connie were sitting around the breakfast table deciding what to do. Arthur and Kirstin only had a few days left in their vacation, and Connie insisted that these be used well. Also, his knee had improved to the point where he could walk normally so long as he wore a brace.

"How do you feel about heading to Yosemite for a couple of days?" he asked. "I ruined our last trip when I fell down the side of that pit, and I'd like to make it up to you."

"Cool!" said Arthur enthusiastically. "When do we leave?"

"It's a Saturday, so reservations may be a problem," said Connie thoughtfully, "but I'll bet I can get us in somewhere. Besides, I never really unpacked from last time." He shrugged. "We can go whenever you two are ready."

"I can be ready in about half an hour," said Arthur. He had been looking forward to a Yosemite trip the whole time they had been in California, and now they were *finally* going to get to go.

Kirstin was excited too, but she suddenly realized that if they went to Yosemite now for two days, they would only have about half a day to solve the mystery when they got back. "Actually, there's something I'd like to take care of before we go, but I'm pretty sure it won't take more than an hour or so. How about I head out after breakfast and we can finish making plans over lunch?"

Connie looked at her. "What exactly do you want to do?"

She hesitated, then said, "I'd just like to take a walk down the Embarcadero and stop in one or two places downtown."

Connie's smile was full of good-natured suspicion. "OK, let's try this again: What *exactly* do you want to do?"

"I'd like to stop by the Maritime Records Repository," she admitted.

"Why?" Connie asked skeptically.

"I'd like to ask the man who works there a few more questions. He said some things that made it sound like he knew more about the *Anna Daley* than just where her records were kept."

"I'm a little worried about your safety after some of the things that have happened on this visit," replied Connie. "Your investigation is over, but that doesn't necessarily mean whoever was after you will leave you alone now."

"The police will be tailing Carlos at least until we leave," said Kirstin. "He'll probably know that, so he's not likely to try anything. Besides, it's daylight and I'll be walking along busy streets in a good neighborhood."

Arthur didn't like the sound of this. He did *not* want his sister doing something that would cancel their Yosemite trip again. Also, his close encounter with the sharks had dampened his enthusiasm for this case. He didn't want to give up, but he also didn't want to have something like that happen again. "Yeah, but you don't know if Carlos had friends," he said using his big-brother-taking-care-of-little-sister voice. "Going out by yourself sounds kind of dangerous to me."

Kirstin started to get mad, but stopped herself and gave her brother a big smile. "That's a good point, Arthur. I'll be much safer if you go with me. Thanks!"

Connie nodded. "I agree. You should be fine if you head out together," he said. "Keep your eyes open and make sure your cell phone is on so you can call the police if you get in any trouble. I'll stay here and make our reservations."

"But will we have time?" asked Arthur. "I mean, I've still got to pack."

"We'll want to leave in about two hours," replied Connie, "so if you two can be back in an hour and a half or so, it shouldn't be a problem."

Arthur decided not to protest further. He had learned from years of experience that Kirstin had an amazing ability to get adults on her side whenever she and Arthur disagreed in front of them. The best thing he could do now would be to head out with her and make sure they both got back in the next hour and a half. He sighed. "OK."

"We'll be fast!" Kirstin assured him. She quickly headed for the door before her uncle or brother could get second thoughts.

CHAPTER 19

THE BURIED SHIPS OF SAN FRANCISCO

When Arthur and Kirstin stepped into the Maritime Records Repository, they had the eerie feeling that they had never left. The air had the same old attic smell, the rooms had the same dim, shadowy light even though it was a bright morning outside, and the same old man was sitting behind the counter working on a crossword puzzle. Even the shirt he was wearing looked suspiciously like the one he had worn before. The man looked up and said, "Well, what can I do for you?"

"Hi," said Kirstin. "We were in here last week looking for records on the *Anna Daley*, but one of her logbooks was missing. Do you know if anyone returned it?"

"Not that I remember," replied the man, "though that don't mean much nowadays. You're welcome to head in and dig around if you like." He gestured to the door leading down into the Crypt.

Arthur and Kirstin headed in and dug around, but ten minutes later they were standing in front of the clerk's desk again. "It's still missing," reported Arthur.

He shrugged and raised his bushy white eyebrows.

"Oh well. 'When books grow legs, they walk away oftener than they walk back,' I always say. Is there anything else I can do for you kids?"

"Actually, there is," said Kirstin. "The last time we were here, you said that the *Anna Daley* had been 'landfilled.' What did you mean?"

"Pretty much everything between the water and the bottoms of the hills used to be ocean," he explained, "but they filled it in a long time ago so the City would have more room to grow. Well, they dumped in just about whatever they could find, and they even used dozens of the old ships along the coast as fill. Some people say there are twenty, some say there are thirty or forty, but nobody really knows.

"Anyway, the *Anna Daley* was one of those landfilled ships. In fact, I was just thinkin' about her the other day. Now why was that?" He wrinkled his wrinkly forehead and stopped for a few seconds. Then he snapped his fingers. "That's it—they just dug her up!"

"Dug her up?" said Arthur.

"They're doing some construction work on the foundation of this warehouse, see, and they found a buried ship. There was a little something about it in the shipping papers two or three days ago. *They* said it was the *General Harrison*, but *I* knew it was the *Anna Daley*," he said with a satisfied smile.

"How did you know it was the *Anna Daley*?" asked Arthur.

"Because that's where she's buried," the man explained.

"Sure," said Kirstin. "But how did you find out she was buried there?"

That was a harder question, and the clerk searched his memory for a while before answering. "That takes me way

back. Let's see, I was in town after the first . . . no, the second
. . . time I shipped out. I met this old-timer who had worked
on the landfill when he was young, and he took me around
and showed me where each ship was buried and he told me
her story." He paused again, lost in memory. "Now that was
somethin'. I bought him lunch just so I could keep listening to
his stories. Did you know there's ships down there from all
over the world? Why—"

"Wow! So we could just walk over and see the *Anna Daley*?"
interjected Kirstin, trying tactfully to keep him on the subject.

"Well, you *could*, I suppose," he said, "but it's not the kind
of thing I'd do."

"Why is that?" asked Arthur.

"For one thing, I don't hold with poking around the bones
of old ships. Seems kind of like rummaging around someone's
grave to me. But then I'm an old sailor and you're not, so I
can't exactly expect you to feel the same way."

"I understand," said Arthur. "We'd do our best to be re-
spectful. Is there any other reason not to go and at least look at
her?"

The old man looked from side to side as if he was afraid he
was being watched, then he leaned forward across the counter
and whispered, "I wouldn't even set eyes on that ship if I were
you—she's *cursed!*"

CHAPTER 20

THE CURSE OF THE
ANNA DALEY

"Cursed?" asked Arthur. He found that he was whispering too.

The old man nodded gravely. "I'll tell you what the old-timer told me. Bill O'Brien was the captain of the *Anna Daley*, and he was a greedy man. He had been taking millionaire miners back and forth between San Francisco and the gold fields for a couple years, and he got more and more jealous of 'em. He got to thinking about their gold day and night until it was always on his mind. He thought about going prospecting himself, but he'd seen enough broken-down prospectors to know better.

"So one day this one-legged prospector gets on board with a whole chest full of gold. Captain O'Brien can't take his eyes off it. All that gold, and the one-legged prospector is all by himself. That night, O'Brien is drinking whiskey in his cabin and thinking about how it's not fair that the prospector has all the luck and all the gold and he—a hardworking ship's captain—has nothing.

"So he goes up on deck to get some fresh air and clear some of the whiskey fumes out of his head, and who does he see?"

He paused for dramatic effect. "The prospector! There he is just standing at the rail on his one leg looking at the stars in the sky and singing a song. And he's been drinking too; there's a whiskey bottle in his hand and it's almost empty.

"And Captain O'Brien, he thinks to himself how it wasn't safe for the prospector to be standing so close to the edge of the deck like that, especially since he's drunk. Then a terrible idea comes into the Captain's heart and all at once he decides what to do. He walks across the deck real quiet like, until he's right behind the prospector. Then he turns and 'accidentally' bumps the prospector with his elbow. The prospector loses his balance and screams as he falls overboard into the black, cold water. There's a splash and then a few seconds later a call for help, but it's already behind the *Anna Daley*, and the Captain knows how hard it is to find a lost man in the dark. So he sails on and doesn't try to go back for the prospector.

"Then he goes back to his cabin and takes out the ship's log. He puts in an entry: *Passenger lost at sea at night.* Then he takes out the manifest, and he crosses out the listing for the prospector's chest of gold. And he goes down into the hold and picks up the chest and brings it up to his cabin. The chest is heavy and he isn't a young man anymore, but he manages.

"The next morning, he's sick. Maybe it was the drink and the hard work from the night before. Maybe it was the typhoid fever." The old man shrugged his skinny shoulders. "Maybe it was his conscience gnawing away at him.

"Anyway, by evening he's hot as a kettle and delirious. Some of his crew try to help him. They bring some cold water and a cloth for his head to try to bring down his fever. One of them pulls out the prospector's chest to sit on, and Captain O'Brien starts screaming. He yells at them to take their dirty paws off his property or he'll tear them apart with his bare hands. Then he says that—" He stopped himself and glanced at Kirstin. "Well, I won't repeat what he said in front of the young lady, but he swore a terrible oath that anyone who so much as looked at that chest would die.

"He died that night. The *Anna Daley* was only a few hours out of San Francisco, but his crew buried him at sea 'cause they were afraid that they might catch whatever had killed their captain. But nobody touched the chest. It just lay there in his cabin 'til they got back to the City.

"The ship owner sends over a new captain the day after they docked; an old fellah he got to come out of retirement. The new captain comes on board and tells the sailors to clean out the captain's cabin for him. They do, but no one will touch the prospector's chest. The new captain tells them they're a bunch of superstitious mutineers and says they'll all lose their berths and be blackballed if they don't do as he says. But they won't do it. So he starts to pick up the chest himself. Suddenly he drops it and yells 'My head!' He claps his hands on his head and his eyes roll back in his skull. Then he just falls down dead right then and there.

"After that, no captain's willing to ship on the *Anna Daley*. There's more ships than captains in the Bay anyway, so the *Anna Daley* just sits there at the dock. Since she's not gonna sail anytime soon, the owner boards up her wheelhouse and rents out her holds as storage—sort of a floating warehouse. Then a while after that they buried her as part of the landfill."

"So there's still a chest full of gold on board?" asked Arthur in surprise.

The old man shrugged mysteriously and leaned back. "Maybe. Maybe not. A curse and two dead men'll spook sailors for quite a while, especially since most of 'em wouldn't know about the gold. And since the ship never had another captain and she never sailed again, there was no call to go into the captain's quarters after that, especially after they were boarded up with the wheelhouse. Then they just filled her up with junk when they were getting ready to landfill her and maybe nobody bothered to look and see what's in some boarded up old room. So maybe folks forgot about Captain O'Brien and his curse and his chest, and it's still just sitting there waiting for someone to remember it again."

"But maybe not," Kirstin countered. "I mean, if *anyone* knew the gold was there, don't you think they would have gone in and taken it, curse or no curse?"

The old man smiled and chuckled. "You're a clever one, missy! Sure, maybe someone worked up their courage and snuck in there one night and carried off the treasure. Maybe that happened." He leaned forward with a gleam in his eyes. *"But maybe not!"*

CHAPTER 21

THE OPEN GRAVE

S o now that we've got that taken care of, we'll head straight back to Uncle Connie's condo, right?" commented Arthur as they walked out of the Repository.

"Arthur!" said Kirstin angrily. They still had forty-five minutes before they had to be back. She was about to start arguing, but then she saw the smile on her brother's face—he was just as hooked by the old man's story as she was. She smiled in return. "Yeah, right. After one little detour."

The "little detour" took them into the odd-looking mix of rundown old warehouses and cutting-edge new office buildings that made up San Francisco's South of Market Area, so called for the simple reason that it was south of Market Street, the city's main road. They found an aging red brick warehouse and paint factory at the address the clerk had given them. The rambling old building still said "BAY AREA PAINTS" in huge faded letters on its side, but a big sign in the strip of grass between the wall and the sidewalk said, "Coming Soon: Howard Court—A new redevelopment by Jackson Street Contracting." The sign showed a painting of the warehouse and factory redone as an office building with a trendy restaurant on the first floor.

Construction had already begun, and large parts of the building were covered by tarps or scaffolding. The builders had dug a huge hole next to and partly under the east side of the old factory, and its foundation hung in mid-air, supported by huge hydraulic jacks sitting on the floor of the excavation. Kirstin glanced at the sign and saw that it showed an entrance to an underground parking garage where the hole was.

"I'll bet that's where the ship is buried," said Arthur, pointing to the hole. "C'mon. Let's check it out."

There were no workers at the site and the gate wasn't locked, so they just walked in. Kirstin felt a rapidly growing swarm of butterflies fluttering in her stomach as they walked and slipped down the side of the hole. There weren't any "No Trespassing" signs, but she kind of doubted they were really supposed to be there. Also, she had always heard that it was dangerous to walk around in construction sites. But they weren't likely to get another chance to check out the *Anna Daley*.

Arthur stopped just before they reached the edge of the building. He carefully examined one of the jacks that held it up. "OK, this looks like the release switch," he said, pointing to a large red switch on the side of the jack that would make it collapse if it was flipped. "If we don't touch any of these, we should be fine."

"How about we don't touch anything period, unless it's a treasure chest," responded Kirstin.

"Even better," said Arthur. As they walked under the building, it cut off the sunlight. After a moment, their eyes adjusted to the dim light in the hole and they found themselves standing in a shadowy forest of jacks and beams that stretched thirty or forty yards in front of them. The bottom of the building was at least six and a half feet from the bottom of the hole, so there was plenty of room for them to stand up. The air was cool and had a moist underground smell. The noise from the street faded as they walked further in. Soon the only sounds were their footsteps and occasional creaks from the building above them.

It was quiet, but it didn't feel peaceful. They were walking in the open grave of the *Anna Daley*, and they remembered uncomfortably the old clerk's comment about leaving the dead ship in peace. The shadows around them seemed full of silent, watchful ghosts, furious that their long rest had been disturbed. Arthur felt the hair on the back of his neck rise, as if someone was staring hard at him from behind.

He tried not to think of Captain O'Brien's murderous curse, but that just made him think of it more. The dim light played tricks on his eyes, and he could almost see the dead captain's fever-maddened specter glaring at them from the darkness, ready to protect his ill-gotten gold.

Kirstin saw the *Anna Daley*'s remains first. The old ship's curved wooden ribs suddenly loomed out of the shadows just a few yards ahead, blackened by long years underwater and underground. They looked disturbingly like the bones of some huge, forgotten monster. "There it is!" Kirstin yelled, her voice waking angry echoes.

They both ran over to investigate, their hearts pounding. The *Anna Daley* listed strongly to her starboard (right) side, so that what was left of her deck slanted at a sharp angle, with the starboard side still buried and the port (left) edge several feet in the air. Her wooden deck was rotted away in many places, and in one spot a big cement pipe ran straight through the ship, but at least half of it was still intact. About halfway down the deck, an old wooden structure jutted out, partially buried in the dirt.

Arthur and Kirstin carefully walked around the wreck for a closer look. They could see the remnants of a ship's wheel in one end of the structure, in front of what had once been a window but was now just an empty space with a few shards of glass. The old man at the Repository had said the captain's stateroom was boarded up with the wheelhouse, so it must be somewhere nearby. A little further back, a row of boards poked out of the earth, showing where a wall had once stood. "Look!" whispered Kirstin excitedly, pointing to something in the dirt. Arthur stooped down and picked it up. A bedknob—they had found the captain's quarters!

CHAPTER 22

THE CHEST

"Look at all this junk!" exclaimed Arthur, gesturing to the pile of rubbish that they had pulled out of the stateroom so far. There were soup cans, rocks, wads of old newspaper, chunks of concrete, broken clay pipes, and a whole lot of half-decayed things they couldn't (and didn't really want to) identify.

At last they worked their way down to the floor, which was made of dingy whitewashed boards that didn't seem to have rotted at all. Kirstin squeezed into the hole they had made in the garbage and started handing out armloads of antique trash to Arthur, who added them to the pile. After a few minutes, she called out, "Hold on, I think I found something! Let me dig it out a little more." She handed out some more garbage, then said, "It's some kind of box, but I can't really see anything. Hold on a sec."

Arthur couldn't see his sister in the deep shadows inside the captain's quarters, but he could hear her grunting and straining. "Do you need any help?" he asked.

"That'd be great," panted Kirstin. She climbed out and Arthur took her place. He couldn't see anything, but he felt around and found a large rectangular object half buried in dirt and garbage. He found a good grip and pulled as hard as he could. His muscles strained and his joints made cracking noises, but nothing happened. Then all of a sudden something snapped and the object came free. Arthur fell backward and landed painfully on a rock, but he didn't notice. He scrambled up and helped Kirstin pull the object out into what light there was.

Now they could see it more clearly, and it was definitely a chest. Its wooden sides had once been covered in the leather that now hung in decaying rags from the rusted iron bands that bound it. A large lock—now little more than a big lump of rust—held it together.

The feeling that they were being watched by hostile eyes increased as they stared at the chest. Kirstin couldn't take it anymore and turned around suddenly. For an instant she thought she saw a dark figure watching them from the gloom, but it vanished before she could be sure. "Hello?" she called nervously. No response. Arthur looked at her questioningly. "I thought I saw someone," she whispered, "but I'm not sure."

"Where?" he whispered back.

"Over there." She nodded toward an area where the shadows were particularly thick.

Arthur swallowed nervously and picked up a big rock. "I'll go check it out." He walked slowly into the darkness, eyes darting back and forth. Was someone over there? No, it was just a pattern of shadows that looked like a hulking silhouette from the corner of his eye. Did something move? He glanced over quickly, but saw nothing except shadows and stony dirt.

After several tense but uneventful minutes exploring in the murk, he walked back to Kirstin. "If there was anything there, it's gone now," he said, tossing his rock on the ground next to the chest.

"Good," said Kirstin with relief. "Still, let's get that chest open and get out of here as fast as we can. This place creeps me out."

"No kidding," agreed Arthur. He squatted down in front of the chest and tried to coax its lock open for a few seconds without success. Then he picked up his rock and smashed the lock off.

He and Kirstin eagerly opened the lid. Its iron hinges broke and it fell off, making a booming sound when it hit the ground. Their hands shaking, the detectives went through the chest. They found some clothes that disintegrated at their touch, a stack of books, some papers, a knife in a sheath, a remarkably rust-free gun, and a set of old-fashioned shaving equipment. But no gold.

When they were done ransacking the old chest, Arthur sat down heavily on the ground, painfully noticing the injury to his backside for the first time. "Nuts," he said dejectedly. "Once we found that chest, I could have sworn we had Fernando's gold."

"Maybe there's another chest in there," Kirstin replied hopefully. "Captain O'Brien would have had his own chest, wouldn't he? So when he brought in Fernando's, there would be *two* chests in his cabin."

"Yeah," said Arthur as he thought it through. "Yeah, you're right." He got up with renewed energy. "Come on, let's go!"

Kirstin got back into the cabin and started handing junk out to Arthur again, who added it to the pile that was now almost as tall as he was. It was hard, slow work, but their spirits were high and they didn't notice their aching muscles or the little bruises and scrapes they were getting.

Twenty minutes later, Arthur and Kirstin were almost done searching the captain's quarters. The little room was still partly full of trash, but they now had enough space to simply move it around as they methodically worked their way across the chamber, clearing off one spot after another. They didn't find another chest though. "I guess there was only one chest after all," Kirstin said with a sigh. "So, what do we do now?"

Arthur thought for a moment. "Well, I don't want to stick around down here any longer than we have to. But before we go, let's at least take a closer look at what was in that chest."

Arthur started leafing through the loose papers, which were mostly charts and maps, while Kirstin looked through the books. She found a Bible, some novels with garish covers, and a ledger book with the word "Manifests" handwritten on it in black ink.

She flipped through the manifest book and found that it was filled with lists of some sort, which were very hard to read in the gloom. The handwriting was cramped and sloppy and the ink was faded, so it took her several minutes to realize that these were lists (or "manifests") of the *Anna Daley*'s cargos on her various voyages. Next to each item listed was the name of the person who shipped it and the person who received it at the end of the voyage. There were a lot of items where the names of the shipper and recipient were the same, which Kirstin guessed meant that a passenger had stowed something in the cargo hold at the beginning of a trip and then took it out again at the end.

With growing excitement, Kirstin searched for the manifests for the 1850 trips. There they were! She squinted at them in the dim light, searching for "Montoya," "Franklin," or "gold." She spotted at least a dozen manifests mentioning gold, but none of them listed a Montoya or Franklin as the shipper or recipient.

Then she found an entry that didn't make any sense to her. At first, she thought she was reading it wrong in the shadowy half-light. So she read it a second time. And a third time. She was about to ask Arthur what he thought of it when she had an idea about what the line might mean. A chill went up her spine and her blood ran cold. She read the line very carefully one more time. "Hey, Arthur," she said, her voice shaking. "You better look at this."

"What is it?" he asked as he walked over. But before she could answer, there was a loud groan and a crack from the building over their heads. They looked up just as a chunk of cement crashed down a few feet from them. "Let's go!" yelled Arthur, but when they looked back the way they had come, they saw that the edge of the building had sagged almost to the ground. All of the jacks holding it up seemed to have collapsed.

They heard another crack. Then another. Then came a whole series of cracks building into a thundering roar as a hundred-ton building came crashing down around them.

CHAPTER 23

BURIED ALIVE!

I n here!" shouted Arthur over the roar of falling bricks and masonry. He grabbed Kirstin's arm and pulled her back into the captain's cabin just as a beam smashed down where they had been standing. "Lie down at the bottom!" he ordered as he lay down himself. "And keep your head down!" She flopped down and covered her head with her arms. They could feel the ground shaking, and Kirstin wondered if this was an earthquake.

A huge slab of concrete slammed down on the *Anna Daley*, crushing everything above ground. The uppermost part of the cabin exploded in a rain of splinters that covered Arthur and Kirstin, but they had managed to get below ground level, so they weren't squashed. More bricks, beams, and dust poured down as the building collapsed above them, but the concrete slab acted as a roof over their heads and kept any of it from hitting them.

The roaring and shaking gradually subsided. A minute after it began, the noise died down to occasional rumbles as the rubble settled. "Are you OK?" Arthur asked.

"Yeah, are you?" she responded.

"I'm fine." He tried to get up, but bumped his head against

the concrete that had come to a stop just a few inches above them. "Wow! That was close!" he said as he cautiously felt around him in the total darkness.

"Do you think it was an earthquake?" asked Kirstin.

"I don't know," he answered. "The jacks around the edge of the building all fell down, but I'm not sure if it was before the shaking started or after."

"How do we get out of here?"

"Beats me," said Arthur. "It feels like there's a big piece of cement covering the whole room. It looks like we've been buried alive. And no one knows we're here, so it could be weeks before they dig us out. Since we don't have any food or water, that'll be way too late." He stopped for a moment. "Hey, try your cell phone!"

"Good idea!" said Kirstin. She found her phone and turned it on. The light from its display was surprisingly bright and gave them their first dim view of their surroundings. They were in a narrow rectangular space that looked disturbingly like the inside of a big wooden coffin with a concrete lid.

Kirstin dialed Connie's number, but the signal from her phone couldn't get through the many yards of debris and dirt between them and the outside world. She tried 911 too, but that didn't work either. She had relaxed a little when the bricks had stopped thundering down on them, but now a tense knot of fear began to grow again in her stomach. What if they couldn't tell anybody they were trapped down there? What if it *did* take weeks for someone to find them? What if they had only traded a quick death for a slow one? She tried 911 again. It didn't work. *Dear Lord, please get us out of here!* she prayed silently.

Kirstin was about to turn off her phone to save the battery when Arthur said, "No, wait! Give it here." She gave him the phone, and he held it out in front of him facing backwards, using its display like a dim flashlight. "I thought so," he said. "Check it out!"

Kirstin squeezed beside him and squinted into the darkness. There was a gap between the concrete slab and the wood and dirt in one corner of their little prison. She couldn't see much beyond that, but it looked like the edge of the slab overhung a small empty space with something gray a few feet further back. She also noticed that something smelled bad. "Hey, what stinks?" she asked.

"I'm pretty sure that's a sewer pipe out there," answered Arthur. "The building collapse must have broken it. It looks like it's big enough to fit us. If we follow it far enough, we should find a manhole." As he spoke, several bricks clattered down into the hole. "Let's go!" he said urgently. "Our way out could collapse any second!"

Kirstin hesitated. "Arthur, that's a *sewer*."

"Yeah. And?"

She couldn't think of any better alternatives. "And I guess I'd better get in it fast," she said unhappily. She appreciated the answer to prayer, but she sure wished it wasn't so gross!

Arthur carefully crawled forward, still holding Kirstin's cell phone in front of him for light. Kirstin crawled behind him. The gap between the edge of the slab and the sewer was surrounded by a crazy jigsaw puzzle of brick, timber, pipe, and cement that looked like it could come crashing down if they bumped the wrong piece. So they were careful not to bump *any* piece.

They found the break in the sewer at least as much with their noses as with Kirstin's phone. A beam had smashed a big piece out of the top of the pipe, but unfortunately the beam now lay where the piece had been. "Looks like we're gonna have to move that," said Arthur, pointing to the beam. He studied it for a moment, playing the light over the beam and the rubble around it. "I just hope we don't bring the whole place down on us in the process."

The little rubble cave was about four feet high, so Arthur carefully got to his feet and set his shoulder to the beam. He pushed gingerly. It didn't move. He pushed harder—still nothing. "Could you give me a hand?"

Kirstin tucked the manifest book, which she realized she had been clutching the whole time, inside her windbreaker and crawled up next to Arthur. They pushed together and the beam moved a fraction of an inch, sending an ominous shower of dust and gravel down from the top of the little cave. The detectives exchanged worried looks, but they didn't have much choice. "OK, as hard as you can on three," said Arthur as he got himself into position. "One, two, three!" They pushed with all their might as the beam began to gradually move and the ruins above them gave a loud groan.

Then four things happened almost at the same time. The beam suddenly fell away from the sewer. Arthur lost his balance and fell into the hole. Kirstin grabbed her brother and tried to stop his fall but wound up getting pulled in too. And the rubble above them collapsed with a roar and an avalanche of bricks and dust.

CHAPTER 24

IN THE SEWERS

Arthur got to his feet just as Kirstin splashed down next to him. He heard the roar over their heads and immediately guessed what had happened. "Move!" he yelled as his sister tried to get up. She slipped and he grabbed her and pulled her out of the way just as debris poured down through the hole. Ten seconds later, the rubble pile in the sewer reached all the way from the bottom to the hole on the top, which was higher than Arthur's head, and he was six feet tall. "Whoa!" gasped Kirstin. "I'd be dead now if you hadn't grabbed me. Thanks!"

"No problem," said Arthur, still breathing hard from their narrow escape. "You can owe me one." He realized that they were in total darkness again. "Hey, do you have your cell phone?"

"Un-unh," Kirstin's voice said in the darkness. "I gave it to you, remember?"

Arthur groaned. "And I put it down so I could use both hands to push that beam. Nuts! Sorry about that!"

"That's OK," said Kirstin, who was too relieved to be alive to worry about her cell phone. "I owe you one, remember?"

"Yeah, well it would still have been nice to be able to see down here." He sighed as he felt around the sewer walls. "Oh well, at least there's a handrail and a ledge to walk on here.

That must mean that people come down here to do maintenance and stuff. If we just keep going, we should come to a manhole or something. Things should be pretty easy from here on, even in the dark."

"Hey, Arthur," said Kirstin, "is it my imagination, or is the water rising?"

Arthur felt around with his foot. There had only been an inch or two of water when they first fell into the sewer, but now it was up around his ankle. He suddenly realized what had happened. "All that stuff must have dammed up the sewer when it fell in. Let's get going before the water gets any higher."

They turned and headed upstream as quickly as they could in the inky blackness. They could hear small, shrill voices squeaking occasionally, and Kirstin remembered reading an article once about sewer rats that grew as big as cats and had all sorts of awful germs in their mouths that would infect you if they bit you. She started to tell Arthur about it, but he said he didn't want to know.

The pipe sloped up some, but the water rose steadily. It was up to their knees now, and it was getting hard for them to walk. They slogged on, looking up for any ray of light that might indicate a manhole cover or other way out. "Have one of your hands touching the wall as we go," said Arthur, "so we can feel any ladders or anything that might mean an exit." So they each trailed a hand along the wall, Arthur on the right and Kirstin on the left. But the water was up to their waists now, and they still hadn't found anything.

Then suddenly Kirstin's left hand felt nothing. She stopped and reached over further, but her fingertips met only air. She took a step back and found where the sewer wall ended. "Hold on a sec. I think I found another pipe." She took a few careful steps into it. "It's not as big as that one," she reported, "but it slopes up more."

"Up is good," replied Arthur. "I was getting worried that the pipe would fill up and we'd drown down here."

So they started along the new pipe. It was narrower than the first one and they had to go single file, Arthur in front, Kirstin behind. There was a slight current as water flowed down it into the first pipe, but the new pipe did slope up more sharply than the first one, and the water level gradually dropped as they walked. After about twenty minutes of walking, it was back down to just over knee level, though it rose again if they stopped for more than a few seconds.

"I don't know how much further I can go," commented Kirstin wearily. Wading uphill in total darkness for over a mile had completely exhausted her. But even as she spoke, something was happening that would make her completely forget her tired legs. A mile and a half behind them, the weight of tens of thousands of pounds of water pressed against the pile of rubble that blocked the sewer. Little streams worked their way through and shot out in high pressure jets on the other side of the pile. A grinding sound came from one side as it moved very slightly. Then suddenly the plug burst and the water roared through like a giant fire hose.

"What's that sound?" asked Arthur. He turned and looked back.

"What sound?" asked Kirstin. She took the opportunity to stop and lean on the railing to rest her aching legs. Then she heard it: a distant rushing and rumbling sound. It was getting louder.

She felt a breeze blowing back down the pipe. It smelled fresher than the air they had been breathing, and it was a pleasant change from the stagnant, smelly atmosphere of the sewer. She turned her face into it as it swelled into a light wind.

Then she noticed that the water current was getting stronger. She felt it tugging harder and harder at her legs. A second later, she could hear it gurgling as it swept past her. The gurgle quickly grew to a loud swish, and the water pulled Kirstin's feet off of the pipe bottom. The swish grew into a roar, and if she hadn't been holding onto the railing, the current might have knocked her down.

"Whoa!" yelled Arthur a few feet ahead of her. She heard a loud splash.

"Arthur! Are you OK?" she called, staring helplessly into the impenetrable darkness.

For a second, she heard nothing except the thunder of the water and air being sucked down the pipe. Then she heard coughing and more splashing. "Help!" cried Arthur as the rushing current dragged him past her.

CHAPTER 25

THE TELL-TALE MANIFEST

Arthur!" screamed Kirstin. She flailed blindly in the water for Arthur with her right hand while she held onto the rail with her left. She found something that felt like an ankle and grabbed it as hard as she could. The pull of the water yanked both her arms out straight and grew so strong she was afraid she would dislocate her shoulders. For an agonizing minute and a half it was all she could do to keep hold of both her brother and the rail.

Then as suddenly as the flood had started, it stopped. The water level dropped back to a couple of inches, the wind died down, and Arthur and Kirstin lay in the darkness, panting and coughing. "Are you OK?" asked Kirstin.

Something thumped and splashed in the darkness and Arthur said, "Ow! I would be if you'd stop pulling on my ankle."

"Oops! Sorry!" said Kirstin as she let go.

"That's OK," said Arthur as he painfully got to his feet. "I'd have been in serious trouble if you hadn't grabbed me. Thanks." Something caught his eye. "Hey, what's that?"

Kirstin stared into the darkness. A faint light shone ahead of them. "Let's check it out!" she said excitedly. They hurried along the pipe as fast as they could, always making sure to keep a firm grip on the railing, just in case there were more surprises waiting for them. About two hundred yards ahead, they found another intersection. The light was coming from the pipe to their left.

Squinting and shading their eyes, they walked over and discovered that the light streamed in through a drain in the street above them. And a few feet over from that, Arthur spotted what they were looking for: the dim round outline of a manhole. "There it is!" he yelled excitedly. "Look!" Kirstin looked, and she decided she had never been so happy to see anything in her entire life.

Arthur climbed up under the manhole and pushed the heavy cover off. It moved slowly with a hollow grating sound like the opening of a giant stone tomb. Light poured in, blinding them after spending the last hour in pitch darkness.

They climbed out and found themselves in the middle of a small street. The breeze felt incredibly fresh and exhilarating on their faces. The watery gray light from the cloudy sky left them blinking and squinting as if they were staring into a spotlight. Even the flat asphalt under their feet felt good after the narrow ledges and slimy curved pipe bottoms of the sewers.

They moved the manhole cover back into place and walked over to the sidewalk. The neighborhood looked vaguely familiar, but they couldn't quite place it at first. They were near the top of a hill that had a beautiful view of the Pacific Ocean and the rolling, building-covered hills of San Francisco. Then Kirstin saw an elegant old limestone building a couple of blocks away that jogged her memory. "Hey, that's the Franklin Building!" she said, pointing it out to Arthur.

"You're right," he said. "That means we must be about . . .

two or three miles from Uncle Connie's place. We should give him a call." They looked around, but saw no payphones anywhere. "OK, maybe we should try catching a cab."

"I don't see any cabs either," responded Kirstin. "And anyway, if you were a cabbie, would you pick us up?"

Arthur laughed. "I guess not. We look like a couple of drowned rats, don't we?"

"Drowned in an outhouse," added Kirstin, who was standing downwind of Arthur.

"So what do you suggest?"

"Let's head toward the Franklin Building. If we find a payphone before we get there, great. If we don't, maybe someone there can call Uncle Connie for us. It's Saturday, but somebody may be at work anyway."

"Sounds like a plan," agreed Arthur.

As they started walking toward the building, Kirstin noticed something heavy in her jacket and suddenly remembered the manifest book. She took it out and looked at it in the daylight. Its leather cover was slightly damp on one side, but it seemed to have come through the sewers in surprisingly good shape. "Hey look, I've still got the manifest book," she commented.

"The what book?" asked Arthur.

Kirstin realized she had never gotten a chance to tell Arthur about her discovery. She stopped walking.

"Arthur, you've *got* to see this!"

"What?" said Arthur as he stopped to look at the book.

"OK, these are lists of all the cargo on the *Anna Daley* on each trip. See, here's a list of each item," she said, pointing to the left column. "And here, where it says 'shipper,' that's the person who sent it; and where it says 'recipient,' that's the person who got it, right?"

"I'm with you so far," said Arthur.

"OK, now check out the manifest for the trip starting April 13, 1850," she said excitedly.

Arthur found the right page and looked it over carefully. He stopped when he got to the line that had caught Kirstin's attention and his brow furrowed. "This is the one you wanted me to look at, right?" he asked. She nodded vigorously. He looked at it again for a full minute, thinking hard. It showed an F. Montoya as the shipper and recipient of a little over four hundred pounds of gold, but his name had been crossed out in the recipient column and replaced by "T. Franklin. "But this doesn't make any sense," Arthur said. Kirstin didn't say anything, and Arthur looked at the entry again. An unpleasant possibility occurred to him and he got a sick feeling in the pit of his stomach. He looked up at Kirstin. "You don't think . . . " he let his voice trail off, not wanting to complete the sentence.

Kirstin bit her lip and nodded.

Arthur stood stock still as he thought it through again. It wasn't a cold day, but he shivered a little. "Wow! We'll have to tell Michael as soon as possible!"

CHAPTER 26

A MEETING WITH TRICIA

The main door to the Franklin Building was locked, but next to the door there was an intercom with a list of names. They dialed Michael's number, hoping he might be in. "Hello?" said a woman's voice.

"Hi," said Arthur. "This is Arthur and Kirstin Davis. Is Mr. Franklin available?"

The intercom was silent for a couple of seconds. "Oh, hi. This is Tricia. Michael's not here. I was just borrowing his office to do some wedding planning. What's up?"

"We've got some more information about the case for Michael. And we were wondering if we could use your phone."

"No problem; I'll buzz you in. Just come up to Michael's office." Half a minute later a metallic buzz came from the intercom and the door clicked. Arthur pushed it open and they stepped in, but Kirstin stopped in the entryway.

"Arthur, the least we could do is take off our slimy shoes, don't you think?"

"Oh, yeah. I guess we'd better."

The building was pretty much deserted and the air conditioning was turned off, so it was very quiet. The only sound was the soft scrunch of their feet on the rich carpet of the hallway. As they approached Michael's office, they could hear a murmur of voices. They half expected to find Michael talking to Tricia, but when they walked into his office they saw her sitting by herself with her cell phone lying on the desk in front of her.

She looked at them for an instant with her mouth open. "Hi," she said slowly, looking them over. "What happened to you?"

"Well, it's a long story," responded Kirstin, "but it involves us being in a sewer, so we probably shouldn't touch anything."

"A sewer?" asked Tricia in surprise. "No, don't tell me about it yet. I bet you'd like a shower first."

"Oh yeah!" said Kirstin emphatically. Arthur nodded his agreement.

"Well, you're in luck. There's a workout room on the other side of the building and there are men's and women's showers next to it. Also, I've got some clean workout clothes back there, and I'm pretty sure Michael does too. You're welcome to them."

"That would be great," said Kirstin, who was feeling grosser by the minute. "Could you call our Uncle Connie and tell him we're here?"

"Oh, and we've got a report for Michael," added Arthur. "Do you know if he'll be coming into the office today?"

"I'll call them both while you're in the shower," said Tricia.

Twenty-five minutes later, Arthur and Kirstin sat in two nice wood and leather chairs feeling, and smelling, much more human. "Michael won't be in for another two or three hours, but I'm dying to hear how you wound up in a sewer," said Tricia.

So they told her about the legend of Captain O'Brien and

the prospector's gold, how they found the *Anna Daley*, their harrowing escape from the building collapse, and, of course, their adventures in the sewers. "But at least we think we finally figured out what happened to Fernando's treasure!" concluded Arthur. "Or, really, Kirstin figured it out, and I think she's right."

"Really?" Tricia said in surprise. "Tell me about it."

Kirstin opened the manifest book on Michael's desk and explained her theory. Tricia looked hard at the old writing while Kirstin talked. When she finished, Tricia was silent for a few seconds. Then she shrugged and said, "Maybe. That certainly is some creative thinking, Kirstin; I don't think anyone has ever thought of that theory before. I'll mention your idea to Michael when he comes in." Tricia spoke nonchalantly, but Kirstin noticed tiny beads of sweat forming on her forehead. On impulse, Kirstin quickly closed the manifest book and put it in her lap. "Could I borrow that?" asked Tricia with a smile. "I'd like to show it to Michael." She reached out her hand for the book.

"It got a little wet in the sewer, so you probably don't want to touch it," Kirstin said.

"That's OK, I'll wash my hands," said Tricia, her hand still extended. Kirstin glanced down at the hand and saw that it was trembling slightly.

"Actually, I'd like to hold onto it for now," said Kirstin uncomfortably. "By the way, did Uncle Connie say when he was going to pick us up?"

"He wasn't there, so I left a message," replied Tricia tersely.

"Oh, OK," said Kirstin. By now she was mostly interested in finding a polite way to get out of that room. "Well, I'm sure you've got a lot to do, so we won't take up any more of your time. We can just take a cab back to Uncle Connie's building." She got up. "Thanks again for the showers and clothes. That was really nice."

"Yeah, thanks," said Arthur as he stood up. "Is it OK if we use the phone at the reception desk to call a cab?"

"Actually, it's not," Tricia said as she reached into her purse— and pulled out a gun.

CHAPTER 27

THE BOOK AND THE GUN

I'm sorry, but I can't let you leave with that book," said Tricia, pointing the gun at Kirstin's chest. "Give it to me." Arthur and Kirstin stared in disbelief. The gun was big, black and ugly. It looked completely out of place in Tricia's slender manicured hand. "Now!"

It wasn't just what was in the manifest book that Tricia wanted to destroy, Arthur realized, but what was in their heads. The book was only a piece of evidence proving what they now knew. With a cold shock, he saw that they would still be dangerous to her even if Kirstin handed over the book, and that there was a good chance that she would kill them no matter what they did.

He frantically tried to figure out whether he could tackle Tricia before she could shoot Kirstin. He looked down at the desktop for a letter opener or something—anything—he could use as a weapon. All he saw were some buttons and knobs, but that gave him an idea. He surreptitiously flipped a switch and twisted a knob. Then he said, "Wait a minute! Aren't you forgetting something?"

"What?" said Tricia.

"San Francisco Police Department," said Arthur, making sure

to speak clearly and loudly. He paused for a second, thinking of what to say next. "The police know about the car break in, the shark attack, and the building collapse. If something bad happens to us, isn't there a pretty big risk it'll get traced back to you?"

"No," said Tricia flatly. "Now get over next to your sister where I can see you better."

"But why not?" persisted Arthur as he slowly walked over toward Kirstin.

"That's not something you need to worry about, is it?" said Tricia sharply. "Now give me that book!"

"But wouldn't it be better for you if we *sold* it to you and sold our report too?" Arthur said quickly. "That way you don't have to worry about the police or us. Isn't that better than shooting us?"

"I'm not worried about the police or you in the first place." She paused for a few seconds. "But I'll pay you each a thousand dollars for that book and your report. Now hand it over!"

"How about a thousand now and a thousand in one year?" suggested Arthur.

Tricia looked surprised that he was trying to negotiate with her, but she laughed instead of getting mad. "I'll give you $750 now and another $750 in one year if your report stays secret. Of course, if it doesn't stay secret, you're dead."

"Of course," said Arthur. He glanced at Kirstin, whose eyes were full of questions and fear. "Is it OK if we talk about this first?"

"No," said Tricia. "We're all done talking now. Give me the book!"

Kirstin started to hand over the book, but Arthur said, "Aren't you going to give us the money?"

"My hands are full right now," Tricia snapped. She looked at Kirstin. "I'm only going to say this one more time: If you don't give me the book by the count of three, you will die. One, two, three!" Kirstin gave her the book.

"Thank you," said Tricia, but she didn't put down the gun.

Arthur took a deep breath and let it out. "OK," he said. "I'll go give Uncle Connie a call to come pick us up."

"Don't move!" ordered Tricia, pointing the gun at his heart.

"But I thought we had a deal!" protested Arthur.

"You were wrong," said Tricia matter-of-factly. She picked up her cell phone with her free hand, quickly dialed a number, and held the phone to her ear. "Are you ready? . . . Good. I'll buzz you in." She turned off the phone and pushed a button on the desk.

"Who was that?" asked Arthur.

"Someone I think you'll recognize," said Tricia with an amused smile.

Half a minute later, they heard heavy footsteps approaching in the hallway outside the office. Then the door opened. Kirstin's eyes widened and she gasped, "Carlos Montoya!"

CHAPTER 28

TWO ESCAPES

Hi, Kirstin. Hi, Arthur," said Carlos. He had the deep, rough voice of a man who smokes a lot. His face wore an evil sneer, and he held a coil of rope, a roll of duct tape, and a big hunting knife. "Thought the police could keep me away, didn't you? Well, there's never been a tail I couldn't ditch in five minutes if I wanted to." He took a menacing step toward them. "Just do what we tell you and nobody gets hurt."

Arthur and Kirstin didn't believe that for a second, and they tensed for a fight as he walked toward them. But between Tricia's gun and Carlos' knife, it was clear the fight would be short and one-sided. The only advantages the two detectives had were that they were fighting for their lives and that their enemies wouldn't want to get blood all over Michael Franklin's office—the stains would be hard to clean up and even harder to explain on Monday. "Don't do anything stupid," warned Tricia.

A police siren wailed somewhere down the street, and Arthur sighed with relief. He had been starting to worry that they wouldn't come in time. He held up his hand. "And you guys shouldn't either. You're in enough trouble already."

Carlos stopped and his face went pale, but Tricia remained

calm. "Nice try, Arthur," she said confidently. "The police have no idea we're here. That siren is a coincidence. Go ahead, Carlos."

"Want to bet?" replied Arthur as the siren grew louder. "The police have been listening to everything we've said for the last ten minutes, Tricia Franklin." He strode over to the side of the desk and turned the volume knob back up. "Isn't that right, officer?"

"It certainly is," a man's voice said from somewhere over their heads. "Mr. Montoya and Ms. Franklin, your location is surrounded. The best thing you can do is to put down your weapons and wait for officers to take you into custody. Don't make things worse for yourselves."

Carlos stood frozen, his face twisted by fury and terror. Tricia quickly grabbed her purse and pushed the "off" button on the speaker phone. She reached for the manifest book, but Kirstin snatched it away first. Tricia gave Kirstin a rage-filled look and Carlos started toward her. Arthur ran toward Kirstin, afraid that they would have to fight after all, but Tricia said, "There's no time! We've got to go now!"

But Carlos didn't move. "Let's use them as hostages since we're surrounded," he said.

The siren outside stopped abruptly. "There's only one siren, so there's only one car," explained Tricia rapidly. "If we run now, we can make it!" She ran for the door and, after a split second of hesitation, Carlos followed her.

They're getting away! Arthur realized in horror. If Tricia and Carlos escaped the police, the detectives would still be in danger. Arthur decided to try to stop them.

As Carlos opened the door, Arthur lunged and tackled him

from behind. He hit Carlos in the small of the back and slammed his knife hand into the half-open door. The knife flew out of Carlos' hand, and he fell to the floor with Arthur on top of him. Kirstin kicked the knife away from Carlos and picked it up while he and Arthur wrestled on the carpet.

Arthur had the element of surprise, but Carlos was bigger and stronger and had been in a lot more fights. After a few seconds, he managed to twist around and punch Arthur in the stomach. Arthur gasped and loosened his grip for an instant, allowing Carlos to break free. He jumped to his feet and ran down the hall as Kirstin helped Arthur up. "Here!" she said and handed him the knife.

As Arthur ran after Carlos, he could hear the voices of police officers talking to each other somewhere nearby. They seemed to be coming from the lobby, so he hoped they were blocking Carlos' escape. Arthur sprinted down the hall, jumped down the stairs three at a time, ran full speed into the short hallway that led to the lobby—and almost crashed into Carlos, who was pressed against the wall at the end of the hall, listening to the police in the lobby. When he saw Arthur racing toward him with a knife in his hand, he ran out into the lobby with Arthur just two steps behind.

Two policemen were cautiously making their way through the wide, wood-paneled lobby with their guns drawn. They both yelled "Freeze!" when Carlos and Arthur burst into the room. Arthur skidded to a stop, but Carlos kept running—*past the police and out the side door!* The officers glanced at each other, and the younger of the two ran after Carlos. The other one kept his gun aimed at Arthur. "Drop the knife!" he ordered.

Arthur dropped it. "I'm Arthur Davis, the one who called

the police," he explained urgently. "That's Carlos Montoya! He's one of the people who were threatening my sister and me! We got his knife away from him when he heard your siren outside and tried to run." Kirstin ran in just then, as if to prove Arthur was telling the truth.

The officer studied them for a second. "Drop your wallets on the floor and kick them over here." They did, and the policeman picked them up and examined their school ID cards and Arthur's driver's license. He put his gun away and said into his radio, "I've got the two kids. They're OK." He handed their wallets back to them. "Where's Tricia Franklin?" he asked.

"She ran out before Carlos," answered Kirstin. "I didn't see which way she went."

"Me neither," added Arthur.

"We didn't see anyone when we came in," said the policeman. "What does she look like?"

"She's got red hair and I'd guess she's in her thirties. Be careful: she's got a gun!" warned Arthur.

"And she's wearing khaki capri pants with a dark green polo shirt," added Kirstin.

"Second suspect is a red-headed female in her thirties wearing khaki pants and a dark green shirt," the officer said into his radio. "She's armed."

"You're not gonna like this, Tom," a voice crackled from his radio. "Suspect one just jumped in a red convertible driven by a redhead in a green shirt. They're gone."

CHAPTER 29

THE FINAL REPORT

Two hours later, Arthur, Kirstin, Connie, and Michael sat around a table in one of the Franklin Building's conference rooms. Until a few minutes ago, voices and activity had filled the room as the police questioned them all, investigated the crime scene, and used the room to coordinate their search for Tricia and Carlos.

The police had found Tricia's car at San Francisco International Airport. They checked with the air traffic controllers and discovered that Tricia, who was a licensed pilot, had taken off in the Franklin Company private jet about an hour earlier. The plane had disappeared from the airport radar screens by the time the police found out what Tricia had done, so they had no idea where she had gone. She had filed a hastily scribbled flight plan saying she and a passenger were flying to Hawaii, though the plane had enough fuel to reach Japan or even mainland Asia.

Michael had looked sick as he listened to the hunt for his fugitive fiancée and heard Arthur and Kirstin tell the police what had happened. He hadn't said anything except when the police questioned him, and no one had tried to talk to him.

Now the police were gone and the conference room was

suddenly very quiet. Kirstin glanced around the room uncomfortably. She noticed that the dark polished wood of the table reflected them all as perfectly as a pool of deep and completely still water. She looked at Michael's reflection and saw that it was looking back at her. She glanced away, but he forced a smile and said, "So, why don't you give me the report that Tricia didn't want me to hear." His voice was steady, but his face was very pale.

"Are you sure?" asked Kirstin hesitantly. "Maybe we should come back tomorrow or something."

"We've all had a pretty big shock, Michael," agreed Connie. "Maybe tomorrow would be better."

Michael shook his head. "No, I want to hear it now, if you kids feel up to it." He paused and took a deep breath. "I can't tell you how sorry I am. I had no idea that Tricia could ever do something like that."

"It's not your fault," said Arthur. "I don't think anyone could've guessed she'd pull a gun on us. Or that she and Carlos were working together. Anyway, I feel up to giving you our report, and I think Kirstin does too." He glanced at his sister, and she nodded. "Actually, she's the one who figured it out, so I'll let her give our final report."

Kirstin put the manifest book on the table and opened it to the right page. "OK, see here?" she said, pointing to a spot about halfway down the page and turning the book so Michael and Connie could see it.

They studied it for a moment. Then Michael looked up. "OK," he said, waiting for Kirstin to go on.

"See how it says '402 lbs., 6 oz. gold nuggets and dust' and then it lists the sender as 'F. Montoya'? It lists the recipient as

'F. Montoya' too, but his name is crossed out and replaced by 'T. Franklin.'" She hesitated, not wanting to draw the necessary conclusion. "So at the start of the trip the gold belonged to Fernando, but by the end it belonged to Ted."

Michael shook his head. "But that doesn't make any sense. This must be Ted's four hundred pounds. Whoever wrote this down must have made a mistake."

"But wouldn't Ted's gold have been listed too?" responded Kirstin. "That's not just a minor thing like an extra umbrella or something that might have gotten left off or mixed up with someone else's. There must only have been a little over four hundred pounds of gold on that ship, not eight hundred."

"Maybe Ted took another boat but agreed to take the gold off the *Anna Daley* for Fernando because of his missing arm and his bad leg," argued Michael.

"I don't think Ted needed to be listed as recipient if he was just helping Fernando unload the gold," said Arthur. "And if that's what happened, why was Fernando's name written down and then crossed off?"

"Yeah, and Tricia's been trying to get us off the trail ever since we took the case," added Kirstin. "Like when we were in that canyon, I saw this carving on the wall. It was a T and an F with a line between them. That might mean that Ted and Fernando split their claim in half, with the T showing which half of the canyon was Ted's and the F showing which half was Fernando's. I was standing there trying to figure out what it meant, but before I could, she called me over, remember? And she just happened to be standing in front of a hole that I couldn't see, but she probably could. Maybe there's an innocent explanation for all of that, but maybe not."

Michael looked at the book silently for a long time. Then he nodded slowly. "And if there was an innocent explanation for any of this, Tricia wouldn't have pulled a gun on you," he said, his eyes still riveted to the line on the manifest. They were all silent for several seconds. Then he said, "Thank you for your report. I'd like to be alone now if you don't mind."

CHAPTER 30

A PHONE CALL AT MIDNIGHT

Michael Franklin sat in his dark living room looking out over the Pacific Ocean. He had grown up in this house, then moved out after college. Two months ago, he had moved back again after inheriting it from his father. This had been his grandfather's house too, and his great-grandfather's. In fact, Theodore Franklin had built most of it as a fiftieth birthday present for his wife.

Michael had always loved the house. It reminded him of his happy childhood when he would run down its long halls and explore its mysterious attics and extra rooms. When he had friends over, they would camp out on the smooth green lawn outside and watch the ships sail back and forth. Sometimes in the spring they would even see whales migrating north.

As he got older, the house also reminded him of his family. Not just his mother and father, but all the Franklins that had gone before them. The chair he sat in was a broad-armed antique that had always been a favorite of the Franklin men. He had liked to sit in it and look out at the majestic view of the Pacific and feel connected to a long line of honorable men who had sat there before him and enjoyed the same view.

But now the ocean was dark, and so were his thoughts. The founder of his family was a thief and maybe worse. This wonderful old house had been built with stolen money. The woman he loved and had hoped to bring here as his wife was a criminal and a fugitive who had tried to hide the truth from him. Any one of those revelations would have been a terrible shock, but together they left him numb and stunned.

The phone rang, sounding unnaturally loud in the midnight stillness. Michael jumped at the sound, then leaned over to pick it up. "Hello?"

"Hi, Michael."

He was silent for several seconds. "Hi, Tricia," he said at last in a stony voice.

"Michael, I am so sorry. I don't know what came over me today. I was afraid Arthur and Kirstin were on the verge of tearing the company apart and you with it, and I just panicked. I wasn't going to hurt them."

"Then what was the gun for?" asked Michael coldly. "And what was Carlos Montoya doing with duct tape and rope? What was he doing there at all? And why were you trying to keep me from learning the truth about my great-great-grandfather?"

She took a deep breath. "I know I owe you an explanation."

"I'm listening."

"Two years ago, your father asked me to give him a very confidential legal opinion, so confidential that we couldn't even discuss it in his office. He asked me to come over to the house, and I did. He took me into the study, opened the wall safe, and took out an old document. 'I want you to look at this and tell me if it creates any legal problems for the company,' he said. 'Don't make any copies or take any notes. Just have a seat and read it.' So I sat down in that big overstuffed leather arm-chair in the den and read.

"It was a letter from Ted Franklin to his son Thomas, which Ted gave him when he retired and Thomas took over the company. It told the story of Ted's gold, but not quite the way I had heard it growing up. Ted and Fernando started out as prospecting partners, but Fernando refused to do any work around camp. He claimed it was because of his missing arm and bad foot, but he also liked to talk about what an important man he had been before the Americans came, and he made it pretty clear that he didn't think a 'great man' like himself should have to help a young factory worker like Ted do camp chores.

"Ted got sick of it after a few days, and he told Fernando that he would either have to start helping around camp or go prospecting on his own. Fernando flew into a rage and claimed Ted was trying to cheat him, which of course he wasn't. Finally, they agreed to split their claim in half, and Ted even helped Fernando set up his own campsite on his half of the claim."

She sighed. "You can probably guess what's coming next: Fernando found gold on his half of the claim. Ted found nothing on his. Fernando refused to share his treasure with Ted, but that didn't stop him from asking Ted to help him bring the gold back to San Francisco. Ted knew what was likely to happen to a disabled and slow-moving older man traveling alone with a fortune in gold, so in spite of everything he agreed to help and protect Fernando on the way back.

"Then tragedy struck as they were sailing across the Bay. Fernando was out on deck when a sudden storm blew in from the ocean. A wave swept him overboard before Ted or the crew could do anything. They tried to go back for him, but the storm made it impossible.

"So Ted found himself responsible for over four hundred pounds of gold. But he also felt responsible for Fernando's family. Fernando had said that his wife had never worked and wasn't very good with money, and Ted knew that Fernando's oldest child was only fourteen. The Montoyas didn't need a treasure—in fact, it would have been irresponsible to give them one. They needed someone to take care of them now that Fernando was gone.

"And that's what Ted did: he took care of them. He made sure Mrs. Montoya always had enough money to live comfortably. As she and Fernando's children got older, Ted offered them all good jobs that paid a lot more than Fernando had earned. When they had children of their own, Ted gave them high-paying jobs too.

"The letter ended with Ted telling his son to keep watching out for the Montoya family now that he was president of the company. He did, and when it was time for him to pass the company on to his own son, he also passed on Ted's letter. And he in turn eventually passed the company and the letter to his son—your father."

"I went through Dad's safe after his funeral, but I didn't find any letter," interjected Michael.

Tricia paused for a second, remembering the relief she had felt as she watched the letter burn. "I advised him to get rid of it."

"So the letter was a legal problem for us?"

"Not really," Tricia answered. "If you add up all the money we've given the Montoyas over the years, it's more than the value of the gold. Besides, this all happened so long ago that it would be hard for someone to sue. But that doesn't mean they wouldn't try. And if they did, it would be all over the papers and news shows, and that could really hurt the company."

"I see," said Michael thoughtfully. "Why didn't you tell me about this? And you still haven't told me why you pulled a gun on Arthur and Kirstin or what Carlos has to do with all this."

"Let me take those one at a time," answered Tricia in a business-like voice, her confidence growing. "I hadn't told you yet because I knew you were upset about your dad's death, and I didn't want to burden you with this too. I was going to tell you, but I wanted to wait until you had settled into your new role as president and had had a chance to grieve for your father.

"I didn't want those detectives figuring this out and telling you because I was afraid they might not give you the full story, and it seems like I was right. I shouldn't have pulled the gun on them; I just panicked when they came in and told me they'd figured out some of what happened. I was afraid they were about to tell you and maybe other people what they knew without putting it in context. By the way, it wasn't even my gun, it was Carlos'. I made a mistake there and I admit it. I'm sorry. I really am.

"About Carlos—I needed someone to help me defuse the situation as quickly and safely as possible. I picked Carlos because I'd known him while he was with the company, and I thought he was a good worker in spite of his problems. Also, he's a descendent of Fernando's brother, not Fernando, so he wouldn't be able to make trouble for us even if he figured out the full story about the gold.

"But the bottom line is that I'm sorry, and I hope we can find a way to put all this behind us. I love you. And I know we both love the Franklin Company and the Franklin family. That love led me to make some mistakes. I see that now."

"Well, at least now I understand why you did what you did," said Michael, "but I've still got to decide what I have to do. By the way, where are you and how can I reach you? Do you still have Carlos with you?"

She ignored his questions. "What do you still have to decide?" she asked in a suddenly tense voice. "Ted Franklin made the decision for us, unless you're planning to cut off the Montoyas."

"Ted made a decision," Michael countered, "but so did my father, grandfather, and great-grandfather. They all decided to accept what Ted had done. Now it's my turn."

"So that's what you've decided to do?"

Michael looked out at the dark ocean and sat silently for a few seconds. "I haven't decided anything."

"Why don't we talk again tomorrow. I'll call you at eight in the evening, and we can discuss this further."

"I don't know if there's much more about the company for us to discuss, but there are a lot of other things you and I need to talk about. I'll be here at eight tomorrow. Bye."

CHAPTER 31

THE LOST TREASURES OF MICHAEL FRANKLIN

At 7:30 the next morning, Connie and Michael sat on wrought iron chairs on the marble veranda of Michael's mansion. Between them stood a small table bearing the remains of a coffee and muffin breakfast that Connie had brought, correctly guessing that his friend hadn't eaten or slept much. "So, what do you think?" asked Michael, who had just finished describing his conversation with Tricia the night before.

"About Tricia or the gold?"

"Let's start with Tricia."

Connie weighed what to say, then looked Michael in the eyes. "I don't think she ever would have told you about Ted's letter."

Michael's mouth and eyes pinched in a brief, tight frown, but he didn't seem surprised. "Why not?"

"If she had just been waiting for the right time to tell you, she would have said something as soon as you decided to hire Arthur and Kirstin. Instead, she did everything she could to keep you from hearing the truth, even committing crimes that could put her in jail for the rest of her life. She didn't tell you her story until you had already heard Arthur and Kirstin's report and seen the manifest book."

Michael nodded grimly. "That's pretty much what I thought too. She sounded a lot more like she was doing damage control than making an honest confession. But why? Why was she trying so hard to keep me from knowing the truth about something that happened over a century and a half ago?"

Connie shrugged his wide shoulders. "Maybe she was afraid of what you might do if you knew the truth."

Michael sighed. "I have no idea what I'm going to do. Remember how Jesus said 'the truth will set you free'? Well, I don't feel free; I feel betrayed. Betrayed by Tricia, betrayed by Dad, betrayed by all those ancestors I used to look up to so much. To be honest, I even feel betrayed by God."

Connie thought about challenging that last statement, but decided that wouldn't help Michael. "I can't even imagine what you're going through right now."

Michael rubbed his eyes and suddenly felt very tired. "All the blessings I used to thank God for every night—Tricia, my family, my company, everything—were really curses all waiting to strike at the same time. In one day I discovered that my whole life was based on lies and theft. Not *my* lies or *my* theft, but now I've got to deal with them."

He sighed again. "I guess this is one reason why Jesus told us to store up treasure in heaven, not earth. You never know when everything you treasure in this world will be torn away from you."

Connie nodded. "It all belongs to God anyway. I guess we shouldn't be too concerned with what He puts in our hands or takes out of them, so long as we know He's holding us securely in His." He paused. "Of course, that's easy for *me* to say."

Michael grinned. "Yeah it is." The two friends were silent for a long time. The only sounds were the whisper of the breeze over the rich green lawn and the faint hiss and crash of the ocean waves. "But you're right," he said at last. "And what God has put in my hands right now is the hardest decision I've ever had to make. What *is* the right thing to do? Go out and buy four hundred pounds of gold and give it to the Montoyas? Give them all big raises? Or did this all happen so long ago that there's really no point in doing anything?"

"I don't know," said Connie. "That's between you, the Montoyas, and God. The only piece of advice I can give you is to try not to think about the cost of doing God's will. What would be the right thing to do if this only involved ten dollars and the Franklin reputation wasn't on the line? If you know the answer to that question, you probably know what to do."

"Thanks," said Michael, "and thanks for breakfast." He got up and stretched. "Pray for me about this, OK?"

"Of course," said Connie as he stood up. He looked with concern at his friend's lined face and troubled eyes. *He looks like he's aged at least ten years since yesterday*, he thought. "Of course I will."

CHAPTER 32

THE FOUND TREASURE OF MICHAEL FRANKLIN

Connie, Arthur, and Kirstin were exploring the Japanese tea gardens in Golden Gate Park later that day when Connie's cell phone rang. He looked at the number on the caller ID and turned on the phone. "Hi. . . . Sure. . . . Of course we'll be there. . . . OK, see you then." He clicked off the phone and turned to his niece and nephew. "That was Michael. He's calling a special board meeting of the Franklin Company for five o'clock this evening, and he'd like us to come."

"Did he say anything more about it?" asked Kirstin.

"No," answered Connie, "but we'll find out soon enough."

At 5:00, they sat in the same conference room they had been in yesterday. Olivia was there too, and so were two men in gray suits whom none of them knew. The older of the two was tall—even taller than Connie—and loomed over the table like an old tree. The younger suit wearer was a thin-faced man about Connie's age who wore glasses and carried a large brief-case.

Michael stood up. "As president, sole director, and sole share-holder of the Franklin Company, I hereby call this meeting to order," he said. He looked haggard and his voice was rough, as if he was coming down with a cough. But his eyes were bright and clear. "Thank you for coming on such short notice. I don't think all of you know each other, so I'll make some brief introductions. This is Connie Hoghton, the Franklin Company's outside accountant; these are Arthur and Kirstin Davis, the two detectives whose work is the reason for this meeting; these are Mr. Doyle and Mr. Wayne, the company's attorneys"; he paused for an instant, "and this is Olivia Montoya.

"I called this meeting for two reasons. First, I wanted to say that, through Arthur's and Kirstin's efforts, the lost treasure of Fernando Montoya has now been found." Olivia's jaw dropped and she stared at him with wide eyes. "It's here," he continued, gesturing at the room around them, "in this building, this company.

"Theodore Franklin never found any gold, Fernando did. And by the time he did, he and Ted were no longer partners. So where did my great-great-grandfather's gold come from?" He grimaced. "He stole it from Fernando." Olivia went gray as the blood drained from her face in shock. Then she turned red with rage as Michael kept talking. "The great Ted Franklin was a thief. When Fernando died in an accident, Ted took his gold and used it to found this company. That gave him a guilty conscience, so he offered jobs to Fernando's relatives and took care of his widow."

He paused, and the room was utterly silent as they all watched him. "What do we do now, a century and a half later? Or really, what do I do now, since I'm the sole shareholder of the Franklin Company? That's the second reason for this meeting. Ever since I found out the truth yesterday, I've been wondering how to answer that question.

"I thought about doing nothing—like my father, grand-father, and great-grandfather—but then I would be no better than Ted. He built his fortune on stolen money, and if I just accepted it and did nothing, I would also be accepting his stealing.

"I also thought about giving the Montoya family four hundred pounds of gold, or at least the amount of money it would take to buy it. But that wouldn't really be fair either because it wouldn't make up for all the years that my family had the money and theirs didn't. I considered paying a hundred and fifty years' worth of interest on the money to make up for all that time, but I realized I couldn't raise that much money without destroying the company, which I don't think anyone wants.

"Also, it would be hard to pick a number to write a check for because I had no way of knowing what the Montoyas would have done with the treasure. Ted thought they would have wasted it, which is one justification he claimed for not giving it to them. Maybe they would have. Or maybe they would have used it to buy land in Marin County and become the richest family in California. Or maybe they would have used it to found a bicycle company.

"I don't know what the Montoyas would have done, but I do know what the Franklins did, with the help of the Montoyas. We took that gold and turned it into the finest bicycle company in America." His voice became unsteady and he stopped. He looked down for a few seconds, swallowed hard, and wiped his eyes. Then he looked at Olivia, who sat as still as stone staring at him. "This is Fernando's treasure, and the Montoyas are its rightful owners."

Michael sat down heavily and nodded to Mr. Doyle, the

taller and older of the two attorneys. "Mr. Franklin has asked us to prepare documents transferring ownership of the Franklin Company from himself to Olivia Montoya and those of her relatives entitled under California law to inherit from Fernando Montoya," the lawyer said in a deep, slow voice that filled the room. As he spoke, Mr. Wayne took papers out of his briefcase and handed them to Olivia, who looked in disbelief at the stock certificates, deeds, and other legal documents showing that she and her family now owned the Franklin Company and all of its property, even the house where Michael lived. As his last act before giving up his stock, Michael had made Olivia the president and sole director of the company.

After a few minutes, Mr. Doyle stopped talking and Mr. Wayne ran out of paper to give Olivia. The room was suddenly very quiet. Michael cleared his throat. "That pretty much covers it. Connie, Mr. Doyle, and Mr. Wayne can help you with any legal or financial questions you have about the company, Olivia. For the next few days, I'm going to be busy clearing out the president's office and moving, but I'll be available to help you get settled in as the new president and . . . and I guess that's it."

"Thank you," said Olivia slowly. "I . . . I don't know what to say. I feel mad, happy, and sad all at the same time." Her voice trailed off. Then she suddenly realized what they were all waiting for. "Oh, I'm the president and director now, aren't I? The meeting is over, uh, adjourned."

The conference room emptied quickly, without the chatting and small talk that usually follows meetings. Connie spotted

Michael in the parking lot and walked over to him. "I just wanted you to know that I've never been prouder to be your friend than I am today," he said. "I know what you gave up, and I know how much it meant to you. But the earthly treasure you just walked away from is nothing compared to the treasure you've stored up in heaven."

CHAPTER 33

HOW TRICIA TOOK THE NEWS

At eight o'clock that evening, Michael was in the kitchen of the house that used to be his, packing his belongings. He was less than halfway done with the cabinets, but he had already filled fifteen large boxes in that room alone. He would never have guessed that even his whole kitchen had that much stuff in it.

He knew he would miss the house and the company, and it would be a long time before he could see a Franklin bike without feeling a pang of regret, but he also felt a deep and surprising peace. He had prayed about his decision and had done what he knew was right, even though it had hurt him terribly. Now it was over. He felt that his soul had been in a refiner's fire and was now bathed in springs of living water. He was physically exhausted and emotionally drained, but he felt spiritually refreshed and even happy.

The phone rang, and he quickly put down the water glasses he had been packing. He flopped down in a chair and picked up the phone, happy to have an excuse to stop working for a little while. Then he glanced at the clock and realized who it must be. He winced; this wasn't going to be pleasant. "Hello?" he said, trying to keep his voice calm.

"Hi, Michael."

"Hi, Tricia."

"Listen, the police may be bugging your phone, so we've only got a few minutes. I know you'll need time to decide what to do about the Montoyas, but in the meantime we'll need to persuade Arthur and Kirstin not to say anything to Olivia. I can't talk to them, of course, but if you tell them that—"

"That won't be necessary," he said, cutting her off.

Silence. Then a sharp "Why not?"

"Because Olivia knows everything. I told her myself about three hours ago, just before I gave her the company."

Tricia gasped. "You're joking, right?"

"No joke. In fact, I was packing up the kitchen when you called." He took a deep breath and let it out. "Why don't you come back now and turn yourself in before things get worse for you? It's over. It's all over."

"Oh no it's not!" she spat, her voice filled with a venom and cold rage Michael had never heard before. "This is most definitely not over!"

"What do you mean?" he asked warily, but the line was already dead.

"If we don't leave in the next ten seconds, we'll miss the ferry," Connie announced as he and Arthur stood by the doorway of his apartment, "and that's the last one that'll get us there in time." He was taking them across the San Francisco Bay to Tiburon to watch the sailboat races that started each summer evening as the sun set and the wind turned and blew steadily out to sea. He knew a little café that offered a terrific view of the brightly colored sailboats skimming across the waves and also served the best ice cream in Marin County. But they weren't going to see the race or taste the ice cream unless Kirstin got out of the bathroom *immediately*.

"I'm coming!" she called as she burst out of the bathroom and ran toward the door. The phone rang just as she passed it. "Should I get that?" she asked.

"We don't have time," Connie answered. "Whoever it is can leave a message." He hustled Arthur and Kirstin out the door and to the ferry, which they barely caught.

Back in the empty apartment, the phone rang four times before the answering machine picked it up. "Hi, you have reached Connie Hoghton," its mechanical voice announced. "I'm not here right now, but if you leave your name, phone number, and a short message at the beep, I'll get back to you as soon as possible. Thanks!"

The machine beeped, and then Michael's voice said, "Hi, it's Michael. Give me a call as soon as you get this. I just talked to Tricia, and she didn't take the news well. I'm worried that she might do something extreme. The FBI hasn't caught her or Carlos trying to come back into the country, so they're probably thousands of miles away. Still, I'm going to call the police, but I figured I'd tell you first. I'm going to try your cell phone too, so ignore this message if I've already talked to you." Five seconds later, Connie's cell phone rang in his kitchen where he had left it to recharge.

The sun hung low and heavy in the west, turning the Bay into a sheet of red gold, broken by the sharp prows of the sailboats as they rounded the last curve of the race. A graceful catamaran with a bright blue and yellow sail was in the lead, one of its two hulls lifted out of the water by the wind and the speed of the turn. Arthur, Kirstin, and Connie had all picked boats at the beginning of the race, and the catamaran was Kirstin's. "Hey, Arthur, look—mine's even farther ahead now," she said as the boats came out of the turn and headed for the finish line.

"Really? I hadn't noticed," said Arthur, who had jokingly pretended to stop watching the race after it became clear that his boat (a sleek yacht that looked fast but wasn't) would probably come in dead last, which it did.

After the race, Connie bought a big macadamia nut cookie as a victory prize for Kirstin, and she shared it with him and Arthur. They also all got hot chocolate to keep them warm on the way home. The evening fog was coming in now that the sun was down, and the ferry ride back would be chilly.

They chatted happily as they left the café and started down the steeply sloping street that led to the ferry dock. Arthur and Connie started talking about sports, so Kirstin started window shopping in the cute—and expensive—little shops lining the streets. Soon she was a few paces behind them, though neither she nor they noticed. Then she stopped for a few seconds to look at a sweater, and when she began walking again she had lost sight of her brother and uncle in the thickening mist. She wasn't worried though; they had plenty of time and the dock was straight down the street.

The fog grew heavier as they got lower and closer to the water. Soon it was as if they were walking in a cloud. By the time Connie and Arthur reached the dock, they could hardly see the beach a few feet below them. The lights on the pier were nothing but soft, glowing balls in the mist. "Wow, this fog is even thicker than the stuff that came out of the dry ice machine you guys used when you put on *MacBeth*, isn't it?" Arthur commented, referring to the play Kirstin's class had performed just before school let out. She didn't respond. "Kirstin?" Still nothing. Sudden panic seized him. "KIRSTIN!" he yelled.

CHAPTER 34

$52,500,000

Kirstin woke slowly. The first thing she noticed was that her head felt funny, like she couldn't wake up all the way. She heard voices talking nearby. They sounded blurry for some reason, and she had trouble understanding what they were saying. Something made of cloth was covering her eyes, and she couldn't seem to get it off by moving her head. Her hands were stuck, so she couldn't reach up to uncover her eyes. She tried to call for help, but she was so weak and her throat was so dry that only a quiet croak came out.

She heard footsteps coming toward her. "She's coming around," said a familiar woman's voice. "Try feeding her now."

Someone poured something sweet and wet into her mouth. Kirstin discovered that she was ravenously hungry and desperately thirsty, but she had trouble swallowing. She choked and then coughed hard, spraying liquid everywhere. A man's voice squawked indignantly a couple of feet in front of her. "That's it! If you want her fed, do it yourself!"

"Let's try letting her feed herself," said the woman's voice. "Take off her blindfold and unlock the cuffs on her hands. She won't go anywhere, not with cuffs on her ankles and that much medication in her blood."

Kirstin felt someone doing something with her hands. Then the cloth was roughly pulled from her eyes. She opened them, but quickly shut them again because the light was painfully bright. She blinked and squinted and gradually was able to make out her surroundings. She was half sitting, half lying in a big armchair. Carlos Montoya was sitting in front of her holding a pink can that said "Balanced Nutritional Drink: Strawberry." Droplets of pink liquid stained his shirt and clung to his hair. Tricia stood in a doorway about five feet behind him. They were in a small room with a wood floor and wood-paneled walls. One wall had a window, but the blinds on it were completely shut. Carlos put the can on a small table by her chair and said, "Drink this."

Kirstin's hands were still numb and tingly from the handcuffs, so she had to be careful not to drop the can or spill. She drank the whole can, then drank another that they gave her. She felt better after that, though her head was still full of cobwebs and she couldn't think clearly. She knew vaguely that she should try to escape or call for help, but she couldn't make her brain work well enough to figure out a plan.

She struggled to remember how she had gotten here. She remembered a boat race and hot chocolate, then being on a ferry—no wait, that came before the boat race. There was something about fog and shopping . . . yes, that was it. And then a large, strong hand suddenly clamped over her mouth before she could scream. Then someone pinned down her arm and she felt a sting in her shoulder. After that, everything faded into darkness and troubled dreams.

She could hear Tricia's voice talking somewhere outside of the room. "Is she done eating?" Carlos said something Kirstin couldn't quite catch. "Good, she should last for at least another day now. Go knock her out again; I don't want any distractions while I'm on the phone."

"It's time to make the ransom call, then?" asked Carlos.

"It's time," confirmed Tricia. "They've had a day and a half to get desperate. They should be willing to do whatever it takes to get her back by this point."

Carlos came back into the room carrying a syringe. He walked over to Kirstin, who tried to push the needle away. Carlos easily overpowered her, saying "Now, now. If you fight, you'll just make this hurt." He trapped her left arm, stuck the needle into her vein, and pushed down the plunger on the syringe. A minute later, Kirstin's vision dimmed and she slipped back into unconsciousness.

The phone rang. Michael glanced at the caller ID, but it read "Blocked Call," meaning that the caller was intentionally hiding his or her number. He picked up the receiver. "Hello?"

"Hello, Michael," said Tricia.

"Do you have Kirstin?" Michael asked, his heart pounding.

"We do," Tricia replied. "And yes, she's safe. For now."

Relief flooded through Michael. For the last thirty-six hours, no one had known what had happened to Kirstin. Since there hadn't been a ransom demand, they had begun to fear that she had been murdered or had gotten lost in the fog, fallen down one of Tiburon's steep shoreline slopes, and drowned. Divers were already searching the San Francisco Bay for her body. "What do you want?" he asked.

"$52,500,000," Tricia said flatly. "When you have the money ready, I'll tell you where and how to send it."

Michael was stunned. "You know I don't have that kind of money. I never did. That's more than the total worth of the company."

"No, it's not. The real estate the company owns downtown is undervalued on the books. In fact, $52,500,000 is the exact net worth of the Franklin Company. You have seventy-two hours to sell it and give me the money."

"But I don't even own the company!" Michael protested.

"Then Olivia had better sell it fast if she doesn't want Kirstin's blood on her hands."

"You can't just sell a company like a used car!" Michael said, agitation filling his voice. "It takes time!"

"I know," said Tricia calmly. "That's why I'm giving you seventy-two hours."

"But—" started Michael, but she had hung up already.

CHAPTER 35

SEVENTY-TWO HOURS

So I gave the company to the Montoyas, and now she's trying to take it back," said Michael, summarizing what he had just told Olivia, Connie, and Arthur. "Since she can't actually have the company, she wants to force Olivia to sell it and give all the money to her."

"Did the police have any luck tracing the call?" asked Arthur.

Michael nodded. "It came from a disposable cell phone purchased in the United States, but it was routed through Thailand."

"So they're in Thailand?" asked Connie.

"Maybe," said Michael. "The police and FBI can't figure out how they could have gotten Kirstin out of the country. Thirty minutes after she disappeared, security at every airport and border crossing in the country had her name and picture, and they'd already been on the lookout for Tricia and Carlos. So they think Tricia probably intentionally routed the call through Thailand to throw us off. Still, they've contacted the Thai police, and they're helping with the investigation."

"You know her better than the rest of us," said Arthur. "What do you think?"

Michael shrugged. "If there's a way to smuggle Kirstin to

Thailand, Tricia's smart enough to find it. On the other hand, she's also smart enough to figure out how to make a phone call look like it's coming from there."

"We probably wouldn't be much help in Thailand," Arthur said, "but we can start looking around here."

Connie nodded. "Count me in."

Olivia, who had been deep in thought, sighed heavily. "And Michael, I'd appreciate your help in finding someone to buy the company. Just in case."

Arthur and Connie sat in a little Italian restaurant a few blocks from Connie's condo. They had just gotten off the phone with Mr. and Mrs. Davis, who were stuck on their cruise ship. They wouldn't be able to get off for at least another three days because the ship was in the middle of the ocean and wouldn't dock until then. After getting their input, Connie and Arthur went out to get some lunch and plan their hunt for Kirstin. "So, where do you think they've got her?" asked Connie.

Arthur poked at his ravioli. "I think they're around here somewhere. In fact, I don't think they ever left."

"Why not?"

"Because if Tricia had been out of the country when Michael told her about giving the company to Olivia, there's no way she could have gotten back in time to grab Kirstin less than two hours later. Maybe someone other than her and Carlos is involved in this, but I haven't seen or heard anything to make me think so. Also, Tricia would want to be here so she could make sure everything went right with the kidnapping—that's her ticket to over $50 million, and she wouldn't want anybody screwing it up.

"I'll bet what happened is that they flew the plane west until it was off the radar screens, then turned around and flew back so low that the airport radar wouldn't spot them. That way, everyone would think they were a long way away and wouldn't be looking for them here." Arthur paused. "There's just one thing I can't figure out."

"What happened to the plane?" interjected Connie.

"Yeah."

"I can help with that. There are lots of abandoned airfields in California, and some of them are still in pretty good condition. They probably could have landed at one of those without anyone knowing."

Seven hours later, they were in Connie's car, headed for the hot, empty lands of central California. The police officers handling the case liked Arthur's theory, but there weren't enough of them to check every unused airstrip in California, or even very many of them. So the officer in charge of the investigation, a Lieutenant Wong, had asked Connie and Arthur if they would be willing to help, which of course they were.

Arthur held a small flashlight between his teeth so he could hold the map with both hands. It was old (the date in the corner said 1947) and hard to read, but it had been made when all of the airstrips were in use, mostly by the old Army Air Force. As the strips were abandoned, maps tended to leave them off, so newer maps were useless.

They had been to five strips already and were on their way to number six. "Turn in here," said Arthur, pointing to a cracked concrete road that turned off to the right. A rusted signpost stood at the intersection, but any sign it once held was long gone. About half a mile from the main road, they found a small scattering of buildings and junk around a weather-beaten and potholed runway.

They didn't see any planes as they pulled up, so they parked and got out to investigate. Arthur walked over to the partially collapsed hangar building and swept the beam of his flashlight around its shadowy interior. It held nothing but some tumbleweeds and a couple of oil drums. He walked around behind the hangar to what looked like an old airplane junkyard. Rotting tires and broken engine parts lay on the ground and rusted fuselage chunks were lined up along one side of the area like old cars, some of them covered by fraying tarps. Connie appeared around the corner of the hangar. "Hey Arthur, what do you think of this?" he said, pointing to the ground.

Arthur looked down and played his flashlight over the spot where Connie stood. Faint tire tracks led from the runway to the junkyard. Arthur followed them with his flashlight—all the way to a tarp-covered heap behind the row of plane carcasses. Arthur ran over, lifted up a corner of the tarp, and looked underneath. His flashlight showed a plane's wingtip with new-looking paint. "Uncle Connie, could you give me a hand?" he called.

They unfastened the tarp and pulled it off together, revealing a small passenger jet plane. Connie pointed to the ground under the plane's tail. "What's that?" Small red spots speckled the ground. They walked over and squatted down for a better look. Connie reached down and picked up a small, brightly spattered rock. "Looks like someone's been painting," he said.

Arthur shone his flashlight on the tail and saw identification numbers painted on it in the same shade of red that decorated the stone in Connie's hand. "And it looks like that's what they've been painting."

Arthur methodically moved the flashlight beam back and forth over the ground under and around the plane, looking for more clues. They found spots of white paint under the fuselage near the door. "The Franklin Company plane has the company logo right about there," said Connie, pointing to the spot on the plane above the paint drippings. "Nice work, Arthur; it looks like your guess about where they flew was right. Any ideas on where they are now?"

Arthur gazed at the night landscape, thinking. "No, but I'll bet I know where they went when they left here," he said, pointing at the lights of a small town a little less than a mile away. "That's the only place in walking distance from here."

They called Lt. Wong to let him know what they had found, but he had left for the day. "Let's see how much farther we can get before calling it a night," said Connie as he turned off his cell phone. "The closer we come to Carlos and Tricia tonight, the easier it will be to catch them in the morning."

They got back in the car and drove over to the town they had seen. Their first stop was the police station. The officer in charge of the night shift knew who they were from a bulletin Lt. Wong had put out on the police wires earlier in the day about the missing jet. "So you found the plane near here, huh? Congratulations. What can we do for you?"

"Once they landed, they'd be on foot," answered Arthur, "so we think they would've come here to rent a car or catch a bus or something."

"You're probably right," said the policeman. "We're the only town for at least twelve miles in any direction. No buses or trains stop here, so it would have to be a car. And that means my brother, Enrique. He's the only one in town who sells or rents cars. Let's give him a call." He pushed the speaker button on his desk phone and dialed. After two rings, a man's voice answered. "Hello?"

"Enrique, it's Tom. I've got a little favor to ask you."

"You can't borrow the Corvette again."

The policeman laughed. "It's not that kind of favor. A couple of criminals may have bought or rented a car from you in the last day or two. We're looking for a Hispanic man; he's about thirty, six feet tall, and two hundred pounds. The other one is a white woman with red hair who's around thirty-five, five foot seven, and weighs around 135. Does that ring any bells?"

"I remember the woman," said Enrique. "She was in here evening before last trying to rent an SUV. I didn't have any SUV rentals, so she bought one. That's the first time I've had that happen. She also paid with cash and traveler's checks— another first. She said she'd lost her checkbook and credit cards."

"Did she show you any ID?"

"I've got a copy of her driver's license. Want me to bring it over?"

"Yeah, I'll see you in a couple minutes."

Five minutes later, they were looking at a photocopy of a driver's license. The name said "Anne B. Johnson," but the picture showed none other than Tricia Franklin.

CHAPTER 36

CLIFFHANGER

I'm going to go make a couple of calls," Tricia said from the door of the cabin. The mountains all around made it impossible for a cell phone to work unless she made a twenty minute climb to a spot where the phone's signal wasn't blocked. "Make sure to give her another shot, OK?"

"OK," said Carlos from the sofa. He had just spent half an hour wrestling a new propane tank into place outside, and he didn't really feel like getting up again right now. He relaxed into the deep cushions of the couch and put his head back. He decided he'd do it in fifteen minutes.

"Did you medicate her?" asked Tricia an hour and a half later.

"What?" said Carlos groggily from the sofa.

"Did you medicate her?" she repeated.

"Uh, yeah," he said. At least he *thought* he had. He'd certainly meant to.

Tricia eyed him suspiciously. "Are you sure?"

"I'm sure, OK?" Carlos replied irritably, rubbing his stiff neck. Falling asleep sitting up always made his neck sore.

Tricia briefly considered giving Kirstin another shot to be safe, but doing that might kill her. Without a live hostage, they probably couldn't get the money out of Michael and Olivia. "OK. Have you checked on her recently?"

"It's been a while," Carlos admitted. "I'll go have a look." He winced as he got up slowly from the sofa—it wasn't just his neck that was stiff after his nap. He walked over to the room where they were keeping Kirstin and opened the door. She sat slumped over in the armchair, breathing evenly. He took her shoulders and pushed her back into a sitting position. She didn't react, and her head flopped over to one side. He let her go and left the room, shutting the door behind him. "She's still out," he reported to Tricia.

That was close! thought Kirstin as the door closed behind Carlos. When Carlos came in, she had been using a barrette to pick the locks on the handcuffs around her ankles—a surprisingly easy trick the Davises' friend Officer MacGregor had taught her. She had gone limp when the door opened, and fortunately Carlos hadn't noticed the open barrette lying on the floor between her feet.

She felt around on the floor for the barrette. There it was! She slipped it into the keyhole on the cuffs and twisted it around like Officer MacGregor had showed her, praying fervently that no one would open the door again.

Click! The right cuff slid open. A few seconds later, she picked the lock on the left one. The ones on her wrists were a little harder to get at with the barrette, but she had them off in five minutes.

She tried to stand up and nearly fell. The drugs in her system combined with spending over two days in a chair with handcuffs on her ankles made her as unsteady as a baby taking its first steps. She tottered over to the window and pulled back the shade. The moon hadn't risen yet, so she couldn't see much except the black outlines of high mountains against the sky. Fortunately she was on the first floor, so she opened the window and clumsily struggled through. She fell to the ground outside with what seemed to her like an incredibly loud thump, but she heard no sounds from inside as she got to her feet.

The edge of the moon peeked over the top of a crag, giving Kirstin a better view of her surroundings. She was standing outside a large cabin in a small mountain valley. A thick grove of pine trees grew in back of the cabin, and a meadow lay in front of it. Cliffs and jagged peaks surrounded the little valley on all sides. A path led down from the cabin, across the meadow, and through a narrow gap about two thirds of a mile away. A quick mountain stream gurgled across the clearing in front of the cabin, made a small pool in the middle of the path (spanned by a rustic wood and rope bridge), leapt away downhill, and vanished under the base of a cliff.

Kirstin quickly decided to stay out of the meadow and off the path. If Tricia or Carlos glanced out a window while she was making her escape, she would be plainly visible in the growing moonlight. Her best bet probably would be to head into the forest and look for a way over a low spot in the peaks surrounding the valley. That would be slower than the valley path, but also safer.

She set off at a fast walk, which was the best she could man-age. The cool night air cleared most of the drug fumes from her head, but she was still physically weak and clumsy. The back of her neck tingled as she walked and her heart pounded; her captors could notice she was missing at any second, and her trail wouldn't be too hard to follow in the tall grass of the clearing and soft pine needles carpeting the forest floor.

She felt better when she reached a stone ridge leading up into the peaks. They'd have a lot more trouble tracking her on that. She climbed along the ridge as fast as she could. Her foot slipped and she nearly fell, sending dozens of rocks and pebbles clattering loudly down the ridge side. She froze and listened. Nothing. After that, she crawled. It gave her some painful scrapes, but it was better than falling.

After half an hour of climbing, the ridge widened and flattened as it joined the main body of the mountain. On one side, scraggly trees clung to the rock; on the other, the ridge dropped away in a sharp cliff.

Kirstin got to her feet and looked out over the cliff. The moon had fully risen now, and she could see the whole valley clearly. The only way in or out was a narrow cleft in the rocks at the far end of the valley. Through it, Kirstin could see a small gravel parking area that held a lone SUV. A dirt road led away from the parking area, then turned and disappeared from her sight.

She had climbed higher than she thought and was now at least two hundred feet above the valley floor. She had also been slowly going right, so that she had made a semicircle and now stood directly above and behind the cabin.

A light shone through one of the cabin's windows, showing a shadow moving inside. Kirstin leaned over to get a better look. A sudden gust of wind hit her from behind and she lost her balance. She stepped forward awkwardly, and her foot slipped on a loose rock at the cliff's edge. She fell heavily on her back and landed with her legs over the edge. Her head spun and she gasped in pain. She felt herself sliding over the edge, but she somehow managed to flip over and grab onto a crack in the rock.

But her hands were still weak and numb. They slowly lost their grip on the stone as Kirstin desperately tried to pull herself back up. Far below her, she heard the rock she had slipped on crash to the forest floor.

CHAPTER 37

"HOLD IT RIGHT THERE!"

W hy would they need an SUV?" asked Michael.

"The only reason we could think of is that they were headed for the mountains," said Arthur. "Hold on a sec." He covered the mouthpiece of the cell phone and said, "Take the next exit going north." Connie nodded. "The closest place where you would need an SUV is the Sierra Nevada mountains around Yosemite, so we're headed there now," Arthur continued.

"We've got a small lodge up there you can use as a base of operations," said Michael. He gave Arthur directions on how to reach it. "My dad used to go up there a lot before he got sick, but no one's been in it for quite a while. It still should be in pretty good shape, though you may need to stock up on food."

"Will we?" replied Arthur. He glanced at his watch. "If we don't find them in the next forty-six hours, our search is over."

"Good point," said Michael. "Tricia called again, and I made it clear that she won't get the money until we have proof that they've released Kirstin and she's all right. She insisted that we find a way to guarantee that she'll get the money once we've got Kirstin, but I think we can work that out."

"So you've found someone who'll buy the company?" asked Arthur in relief. He'd been afraid that they wouldn't be able to get the money by the deadline Tricia had set, and he didn't want to think about what might happen after that.

"We did," confirmed Michael. "Olivia and the buyer are set to sign the contract at noon tomorrow, though the money won't come in until twenty-four hours after that. She's having her family members sign the necessary papers tonight. They've really impressed me through all this; they're pretty angry and frustrated, but not one of them refused once they understood that Kirstin's life was at stake. They all could have retired comfortably on the money from the company—some of them had already started making plans—but they're all willing to give it up to save a girl most of them have never even met."

"Wow!" Arthur hadn't really focused on the sacrifice the Montoyas were making. He tried to think of something non-lame to say, but he couldn't. "That's really great. I don't know how we'll ever be able to thank them." The phone started to beep to let him know that its battery was low. "Uncle Connie's phone is running out of power, so I'd better go, but we'll let you know as soon as we have any news. And thanks for letting us use your lodge."

The eastern stars were just beginning to fade when Arthur and Connie turned into the dirt road that led up to the Franklin lodge. They had driven all night, stopping only twice—once to rent an SUV so they could go wherever Tricia and Carlos went, and once to eat what Connie called—"dreakfast," a greasy meal at a twenty-four-hour roadside diner that was too late for dinner and too early for breakfast.

They planned to catch a few hours of sleep at the lodge before heading out in search of Carlos and Tricia, and Arthur could hardly wait. He had forced himself to stay awake to keep Connie company so he wouldn't fall asleep at the wheel, but the last hour or so had been sheer torture.

At the end of the dirt road was a place where they could park before making the final short hike up to the lodge. But Connie stopped the car in the middle of the road. *Another SUV was already parked ahead!*

Arthur and Connie were suddenly wide awake. Arthur quickly checked the license plate of the other SUV against his notes from their conversation with Enrique. "That's them!" he said tensely.

"Call the police!" said Connie.

Arthur took out the cell phone, but its battery had completely died. "Nuts!" he said and showed it to his uncle.

Connie furrowed his brows and sat silently for a few seconds. Then he made a mistake. He turned off the headlights and parked the car by the side of the road. "OK, we'll check this out and see if there's anything we can do. They won't be expecting us, so we'll have the advantage of surprise. If we can't rescue Kirstin quickly and safely, we'll head back to civilization and stop at the first place with a phone."

They got out of the car and went around to the back to take out some gear. "Hold it right there!" said a voice behind them. They whirled around and saw Carlos Montoya step out from behind a large tree, grinning widely in the gray morning light. He held a large gun in his hand. He squinted his left eye and aimed the gun at Arthur.

Bang! The harsh echoes of the gunshot reverberated from

the high stone walls. Sudden hot pain seared through Arthur's right shoulder. He looked down in shock and saw a deep, ragged cut where the bullet had torn through shirt and skin. Blood flowed freely down his arm. "That's for jumping me the last time we met," said Carlos. "That's also to let both of you know that there's no one for miles around, so don't even bother yelling or trying to escape."

CHAPTER 38

AN ELECTRIC MOMENT

All at once Kirstin's fingers slipped off entirely and she fell into the darkness. She opened her mouth to scream, but before any words came out, her feet hit something and she landed in a heap.

She got up slowly and saw that she had landed on a small shelf of stone about ten feet below the top of the cliff. Beneath her, a steep pile of broken rock and loose shingle reached from the forest floor almost up to the ledge. It would be impossible to climb up, but she could probably climb down. Climbing down couldn't be done quietly, however, and she would wind up less than a hundred feet from the back of the cabin. Also, she would probably cause a minor avalanche on the way down, and she could get herself hurt or killed if she wasn't careful.

She decided the best thing to do was to wait until morning. Hopefully Tricia and Carlos would go looking for her and she could sneak into the cabin and call the police. Or maybe she could find a safer and quieter way down from her perch. She crawled behind some thin bushes that clung to the rock and curled up to pray and wait for dawn.

She woke to the sound of Tricia's voice. "OK, I'm up on the cliff. I don't see anything yet; how about you?" Kirstin opened her eyes and looked around, moving as little as possible. Tricia was standing on almost the exact spot Kirstin had fallen from, holding a two-way radio in one hand. Her other hand held a set of binoculars to her eyes as she scanned the valley. *If she looks down, I'm dead*, thought Kirstin. She lay in plain view just a few feet below Tricia. If Kirstin had been snoring a minute ago, Tricia would already have found her.

It was still dark, but not as dark as it had been. Kirstin realized that it must be almost dawn. She could see a small figure slowly walking down the path across the canyon, head turning from side to side as it went. It stopped for a moment and raised its hand to its head. "Nothing yet," came Carlos' voice from Tricia's radio. "She can't have gotten too far with all those drugs in her system."

"That depends on how long she's been—Hold on!" She was looking intently at something with her binoculars. Kirstin strained her eyes to see what it was; a tiny light seemed to be moving in the distance. "Headlights!" said Tricia. "Someone's coming! You'd better head down to the parking area and get ready to greet them."

"I'm on it!" replied Carlos. The figure on the path started to run, then disappeared through the gap in the mountains.

Kirstin watched breathlessly as the light got closer and closer. It split in two as it approached and she could hear the faint sound of a car engine. Then it stopped and the lights and the engine noise both vanished. Half a minute later a gunshot echoed up the canyon. Kirstin's heart skipped a beat. Tricia muttered something that ended with "idiot!" She clicked on the radio. "What happened?" she asked.

"I've got Arthur and his uncle," said Carlos. "I was just sending them a little message. Don't worry; I didn't kill anybody . . . yet."

"I'll get the handcuffs and bring them down to you. Then let's take them up to the lodge and see what they can tell us. And don't do any more shooting if you can avoid it; there's probably no one to hear, but there's no point in advertising our presence."

Tricia turned and vanished from Kirstin's sight. Fifteen minutes later, she saw Tricia emerge from the forest and walk briskly back to the cabin. A few minutes after that, Tricia reemerged carrying some rope and two pairs of handcuffs as she headed down the path.

As soon as Tricia was safely away from the cabin, Kirstin scrambled down the rock pile and toward the cabin as quickly and quietly as she could, praying that her enemies wouldn't see or hear her. She slipped into a side door between the propane tank and the quietly humming generator. The door opened into a small room containing fishing equipment and a couple of extension cords, but no phone and no gun. Kirstin hurriedly went through the whole cabin looking for these all-important items, but without success. *Carlos must have the only gun*, she realized, *but where are the phones?* Then she remembered the generator and seeing a hand pump by the kitchen sink. If the cabin didn't have running water or electric lines, it probably didn't have phone lines either.

So what do I do now? she wondered. She only had twenty minutes or so until Tricia and Carlos returned with their new prisoners. Kirstin looked nervously down the path in front of the cabin. She didn't see anyone coming yet, but she *did* see something else that caught her attention.

The handcuffs clicked tightly into place, locking Connie's and Arthur's wrists in front of their bodies. "Now move!" ordered Carlos. They went in single file along the narrow path—Tricia in front, then Arthur, Connie, and Carlos in the back with his gun ready. Arthur's shoulder throbbed with pain, and he was dizzy from blood loss and shock. Fortunately, the bullet hadn't hit any major blood vessels, or he would have been dead by now.

Connie and Arthur both desperately looked for any chance to break loose before they reached the lodge, which they saw was really a large cabin. Once they were inside, escape would be even harder. But their captors were careful, and they didn't get that chance.

They reached the rope and wood bridge in front of the cabin. It was wobbly, and they all had to use their hands to hold onto the guide ropes on either side. Arthur and Connie quickly saw that this would be their best opportunity to try something, but Tricia and Carlos saw that too. Carlos gave the gun to Tricia and crossed by himself while the prisoners waited. Then Arthur and Connie crossed separately under the watchful eyes of their captors. Finally, Tricia crossed, holding the gun with one hand while she held the rope with the other.

When she was about halfway across, something moved in the bushes at the end of the bridge nearest the lodge. There was a sharp thunk! of metal hitting wood, and the rope holding up one side of the bridge suddenly snapped. Tricia tumbled into the water with a loud splash. "Freeze!" yelled Kirstin as she stepped out of the bushes. In one hand she held a camping hatchet, which she had just used to cut the rope where it attached to the post at the end of the bridge. Her other hand—which was stretched over the water—held the end of an orange extension cord. Tricia started to point the gun at Kirstin, but Kirstin quickly said, "Guess what happens if I drop this in the water!"

Four pairs of eyes followed the cord from Kirstin's hand to where it disappeared into the grass, then glanced up to the generator; an orange extension cord led from it into the grass. "If you shoot me or anyone else, the cord falls in the water and you get electrocuted," warned Kirstin.

Carlos started toward Kirstin, but Connie's two-handed blow caught him on the side of the head and sent him tumbling to the ground. He started to get up, but Connie hit him again, his cuffed hands locked together in a sledgehammer double fist. Connie jumped on top of Carlos and wrapped his strong hands around Carlos' throat. "It would be a very good idea for you to give me the key to the handcuffs," he informed Carlos.

Carlos quickly produced the key from his pocket, and a few minutes later he was handcuffed and Arthur and Connie weren't. Tricia still stood in the four-foot-deep icy water holding the gun. Her lips were turning blue and she shivered uncontrollably, but she was unwilling to give up. "Tricia, why don't you just drop the gun and come out?" said Kirstin, whose arm was getting tired. "You can't win. If you start shooting, you'll get electrocuted. If you just stand there pointing your gun at us, you'll pass out from hypothermia. Wouldn't it be better just to stop this now?"

Tricia stood undecided for a moment. Her hand shook so badly from the cold that she could hardly aim the gun. Her face was a mask of helpless rage and frustration, and for an instant Kirstin thought she might cry. But she mastered herself, calmly tossed the gun away, and walked out of the water.

CHAPTER 39

THE RETURN OF MR. DOYLE

The next few hours involved a lot of talking, which started as soon as they reached a working phone. There were calls to Olivia and Michael to tell them the good news and to call off the sale of the Franklin Company, to Mr. and Mrs. Davis to let them know their children were all right, talks (on the phone and then in person) with the police and FBI, and lots of calls from reporters who had been following the story.

Arthur and Kirstin spent most of the afternoon at a local hospital. Arthur needed to have his gunshot wound treated, and the doctors wanted to check Kirstin to make sure she was OK after spending over two days in a drugged coma. They were both fine, though Arthur would have a scar on his right shoulder for the rest of his life. He didn't mind; in fact, he was already thinking up excuses to show it to his classmates (particularly the ones on the cheerleading squad) and tell them the story of how he got it.

They spent the night in a hotel and drove back to San Francisco the next morning. When they arrived back at Connie's condo, the tape on Connie's answering machine was full. One of the messages on it was from Olivia: "Hi, this is Olivia. We've scheduled a board meeting at the company for Friday at five o'clock, and we'd like you to attend if you can."

Friday at 4:58, Connie, Arthur, and Kirstin walked into the big conference room at the Franklin Company, which was several times larger than the room they'd met in before. Seated around the long table were about twenty Hispanic men and women who, Arthur and Kirstin guessed, were members of the Montoya family. Michael was also there, as were Mr. Doyle and Mr. Wayne, who were both wearing blue suits this time. Mr. Wayne had a stack of papers on the table in front of him.

Connie and the detectives sat down next to Michael. Connie leaned over to Michael. "What are those guys doing here?" he whispered, with a glance in the direction of the lawyers.

"I'll bet Wayne is here to hand out paper," Michael whispered back. "I have no idea why Doyle is here." Mr. Doyle noticed Michael looking at him and nodded to him with a knowing twinkle in his eye.

At exactly 5:00, Olivia walked in and sat down at the head of the table. She wore a charcoal gray suit and her hair was pulled back in a professional bun. "Thanks for coming, everyone," she said. "I hereby call this combined meeting of the shareholders and directors of the Franklin Company to order. The first item on our agenda is to vote on the following resolution." As Michael had predicted, Mr. Wayne pulled out a sheaf of papers and passed them around. Olivia took one of them and read:

> Whereas, criminals tried to force the shareholders of the Franklin Company ("the Company") to pay the entire value of the Company as ransom for the life of Kirstin Davis;

> Whereas, these criminals were captured and the

Company saved through the quick thinking, courage, and faith of Kirstin Davis, Arthur Davis, and Conable Hoghton; and

Whereas, the shareholders and directors of the Company wish to express their deep and heartfelt thanks for the actions of these three heroes,

Now therefore, the shareholders and directors of the Company make the following resolutions:

Resolved, as a small token of the appreciation of its shareholders and directors, the Company shall provide Kirstin Davis, Arthur Davis, and Conable Hoghton with whatever Company products they may request for so long as they shall live.

Resolved, the officers of the Company are authorized to take such other and further steps as they deem appropriate to express the Company's gratitude to these three individuals.

"All in favor of the resolution say aye," said Olivia.
"Aye!" said a loud chorus.
"All opposed say nay." Silence. "OK, the resolution is adopted. Let's give them a hand for their great work!" There was a long round of applause, during which Kirstin leaned over to Connie and asked, "Did they just give us free Franklin stuff for the rest of our lives?" He smiled and nodded. Kirstin's eyes lit up with excitement. "Cool!"

After the clapping died down, Olivia said, "Now for the other item on the agenda." She turned to Michael. "You said that this company was founded on Fernando Montoya's gold. That's true, but it was built by the Franklins and Montoyas working together. Without the Franklins, there would be no Franklin Company.

"Ted Franklin was a thief, but you're not. God doesn't punish children for the sins of their parents, and the Montoyas don't either. As soon as you found out the truth, you did what was right even though we know how much this company means to you. Well, now it's our turn. When Ted and Fernando left San Francisco to go prospecting, they were equal partners. We think that partnership should be restored." She sat down and nodded to Mr. Doyle. There was a faint murmur as some of the Montoyas whispered to each other, but Michael, Connie, Arthur, and Kirstin sat silently, hardly daring to breathe.

Mr. Doyle cleared his throat and the room became quiet. "Mr. Franklin, it is my pleasant duty to inform you that the shareholders of the Franklin Company have each assigned half of their shares to you; you now own half of the Franklin Company." Mr. Wayne handed Michael a stack of stock certificates and other documents. "They have also voted to elect you president of the company. If you accept the presidency, they have further voted to give you the right to live in the house in Pacific Heights that has been occupied by past presidents of the company." He paused and looked at Michael, who stared back at him. After a few seconds, he said, "Mr. Franklin, do you accept the presidency of the Franklin Company?"

"Yes . . . yes, of course," stuttered Michael. Olivia got up from the chair at the head of the table and smiled as she gestured for Michael to sit in it. When he did, the room erupted in cheers and applause. Arthur and Kirstin clapped so hard their hands hurt.

When the applause finally died down, Michael said, "I am overwhelmed. I did not expect or deserve this. I honestly don't know what to say other than thank you." He stopped speaking, but everyone kept looking at him expectantly. After a moment, he realized why and laughed. "That's right, I'm the president. The meeting is adjourned."

Arthur, Kirstin, and Connie paused at the top of the slope to admire the scenery and catch their breaths. They had been riding their new Franklin mountain bikes uphill for over half an hour now, and they were pretty high up—and pretty tired. "What a great view!" remarked Arthur. He and Kirstin had missed their flight back and hadn't been able to get another one until several days later without paying an arm and a leg, but they didn't mind—now they *finally* had a chance to visit Yosemite.

"There's El Capitan," said Connie, pointing to a steep cliff that rose out of the pine forests about five miles away, glowing gold and red in the early evening sunlight. "And that's Bridalveil Fall," he continued, gesturing to a spectacular plume of water that jetted out of a gap in the mountains.

"It's beautiful," panted Kirstin as she rode up. "Thanks for taking us up here. It was really nice of Michael to let us use the lodge."

"I'll bet you're enjoying it more this time than on your last visit," said Connie.

"That's for sure!" Kirstin laughed. "It's a lot more fun without Carlos and Tricia." She paused for a moment and leaned on her handlebars. "It's kind of funny—Tricia loved money more than God, and now she's got neither. Michael loved God more than money, and now he's got both."

Connie nodded. "Tricia decided she would rather have treasure on earth than in heaven, and now she's paying for that mistake. But God hasn't given up on Tricia, and neither should we. She and Carlos need our prayers now more than ever." He shaded his eyes and looked along the road they were taking, which headed due west. "Let's get going. We're still about three or four miles from the end of the trail, and it'll be getting dark soon." And they all rode off down the hill.

The Case of the Autumn Rose
The Davis Detective Mysteries Series
By Rick Acker

Paperback • Ages 8-12 • 192 pgs.

Be sure to check out *The Case of the Autumn Rose,* another book of adventures in The Davis Detective Mysteries Series.

> *Arthur was just getting ready to get out of the car when he heard a strangled scream! He crouched down behind the front seat and carefully peered out at what was happening. Three large Asian men . . . with black gloves on their hands were carrying a struggling man out of the bathroom. His mouth, arms, and legs, were bound with silver duct tape.*
>
> *His heart racing, Arthur felt for his cell phone. With a sinking feeling, he realized that he had left it at home.*